Nowhere
BETTER
THAN
Here

Nowhere Better Than Here

Sarah Guillory

Roaring Brook Press
New York

Published by Roaring Brook Press
Roaring Brook Press is a division of Holtzbrinck
Publishing Holdings Limited Partnership
120 Broadway, New York, NY 10271 • mackids.com

Our books may be purchased in bulk for promotional, educational, or business use. Please contact your local bookseller or the Macmillan Corporate and Premium Sales Department at (800) 221-7945 ext. 5442 or by email at MacmillanSpecialMarkets@macmillan.com.

Library of Congress Cataloging-in-Publication Data

Names: Guillory, Sarah, author.
Title: Nowhere better than here / Sarah Guillory.
Description: First edition. | New York : Roaring Brook Press, 2022. | Audience: Ages 8–12. | Audience: Grades 7–9. | Summary: Thirteen-year-old Jillian Robichaux's coastal Louisiana town of Boutin suffers a catastrophic flood that might be too much for her community to overcome, but she is determined to keep both Boutin and its indomitable spirit alive.
Identifiers: LCCN 2022011899 | ISBN 9781250824264 (hardcover) | ISBN 9781250824257 (ebook)
Subjects: CYAC: Floods—Fiction. | Climatic change—Fiction. | Community life—Fiction. | Louisiana—Fiction. | LCGFT: Novels.
Classification: LCC PZ7.G9387 No 2022 | DDC [Fic]—dc23
LC record available at https://lccn.loc.gov/2022011899

First edition, 2022 • Book design by Trisha Previte
Printed in the United States of America by Lakeside Book Company, Harrisonburg, Virginia

ISBN 978-1-250-82426-4
10 9 8 7 6 5 4 3 2 1

For my parents, who gave me stories
and a belief that I could do absolutely
anything if I worked hard enough

Chapter One

If you want to visit Boutin, Louisiana, you drive south until the road runs out. My grandma Nonnie says that road gets shorter every year, so if you're coming, you'd better hurry.

You're running out of time.

And you want to visit Boutin. We have live oak trees that are older than the state itself. Most of them are draped with Spanish moss, which is like nature's version of lace. Sunsets over the marsh set the sky on fire and turn the water a real pretty shade of pink.

My best friend, Maddie, who's also my cousin, liked to point out that we had humidity and mosquitoes too, but that was because she wanted to move to a big city without either.

But I couldn't imagine living anywhere else. I fished whenever I wanted, or shrimped with Mama and Nonnie, or just sat on the back porch and listened to the cicadas.

At the moment I was pretending to listen to Mrs.

Hebert review the formula for the area of a circle. Mostly I was staring out the window and praying it would stop raining already. It had been raining since yesterday, and Nonnie and I were supposed to go fishing after school today. She'd said she'd let me drive the boat.

"Jillian Robichaux?"

I snapped my head to the front. A couple of students giggled.

"If the radius is seven, what is the area?" Mrs. Hebert's tone made it clear she'd asked this question already. "*A* equals pi *r* squared, remember?"

The only pie I was really concerned about at that moment was the pecan pie in our fridge. I was not going to spend the rest of my life sitting in a room working math problems. Being inside all day made me jumpy—made my head hurt and my skin crawl. I breathed better outside, thought better on the move. I wanted a breeze on my face and the wide-open sky.

Maddie mumbled what was probably the answer under her breath, but I couldn't hear over the sound of the sudden downpour. Everyone turned to stare out the window.

"Eyes up here, please. You've all seen rain before."

"Yeah, and we've all seen Mrs. Pitre down at Dell's in her bathrobe," Derek Cannella said. "But if she was in her bathrobe and curlers outside this window, we'd still all look."

I snorted. Maddie looked shocked.

Mrs. Hebert did not get angry. She'd been dealing with seventh graders since God was a boy. She'd taught my mama and Derek's mama. If our parents came through Boutin schools, odds were she'd at least attempted to teach them the area of a circle. She said our parents were responsible for her first gray hairs and we were going to be responsible for her last.

"I'm sure you're right," she told Derek. "Now why don't you tell me what the area is?"

"C'mon, Mrs. Hebert, I can't think when I'm this hungry."

"That's worrisome, since you're always hungry," she said.

"Somebody get that boy a granola bar or something," I said. "Otherwise we'll all go hungry."

The class laughed, including Derek. "Man, that was way back in third grade."

He'd disappeared during spelling and our teacher had found him hiding in a closet, eating out of everyone's lunchboxes. "Yeah, but my nonnie had packed me a couple of pralines that day, so I'm still holding a grudge."

"If anyone should be holding a grudge, it's me," Mrs. Hebert said. "Stop hijacking my lesson."

The intercom rang throughout the school. Mrs. Hebert threw up her hands and we all slid to the edges of our seats. "Attention students," said our principal, Mrs. Melancon. "Due to the rain, we are letting out early."

My shout of joy came flying right out of my mouth. Joy was quick like that sometimes.

Mrs. Melancon paused long enough to let us express our approval before continuing. "School will also be canceled tomorrow."

I whooped again and gave Maddie a high five. Sometimes life was good. Sometimes it gave you days off instead of math quizzes.

"Stay tuned to the local news for updates, though at this time we anticipate returning to school on Friday. If you ride the bus, you need to get to the front on the bell, as the bus is already here."

I swept everything on my desk into my bag. Maybe Nonnie would take me fishing all day tomorrow. Surely this rain would be over by then.

The bell rang.

"Tomorrow's quiz will be on Friday instead!" Mrs. Hebert shouted as we practically sprinted out of the classroom. I couldn't bother worrying about that quiz now. I was going to spend the rest of the day eating pecan pie and trying to beat Nonnie at cards.

We all poured into the high school side of the building like the Mississippi dumping into the Gulf. The walls between our two sides of the building were filled with group pictures of every graduating class since 1942—my grandparents were on that wall, and my parents, and all my aunts and uncles and cousins. Maddie and I shoved our way through bigger kids to get in the bus line. There was no cover, so even though we were both wearing rain jackets, we were going to get wet.

Soaking wet, as it turned out.

The bus was right outside the building, but it still felt like I'd been caught in the washing machine. I dripped the entire way down the aisle. Dripped all over my seat. Realized I would be sitting in a puddle all the way home.

"I can't believe they canceled school over rain!" I said.

The rain seemed to take offense at that. It fell harder.

Ms. Shelby, our bus driver, didn't even bother trying to keep us quiet. The younger kids were bouncing in their seats, and it sounded like the high school kids behind me were planning a party.

"Are you going to your dad's this weekend?" Maddie asked. Her dark hair was plastered to the back of her neck.

"Nope." Dad hadn't asked me to come stay in months. He lived about two hours north and, according to his occasional phone call, spent most of his time working. I spent most of those phone calls pretending I didn't care that he was too busy to see me.

"I'll ask my mom if you can spend the night on Saturday. I think my dad's cooking a jambalaya for the LSU game."

Sometimes Maddie tried to replace my dad with her dad. But she didn't have to do that. Besides the fact that her dad was already my parrain, I had Mama and

Nonnie loving me more than fifty fathers (or godfathers) ever could.

But I sure wouldn't turn down her dad's jambalaya.

The bus rumbled through town. It didn't matter that the rain blurred almost everything outside the bus windows. I'd lived in Boutin my whole life and knew this place with my whole heart. I knew that the gas station was packed, most people getting bread, beer, and fuel for their generators. Mama called that the Louisiana storm kit. Velma Washington, who ran the gas station, probably had two pens in her hair and was looking for her glasses. I knew that the old men who stood outside the Shrimp Shed and gossiped would have moved just underneath its front porch, barely out of the weather and absolutely complaining about it. I knew that most of the buildings needed painting, that nothing new had been built in the last five years, and that, for some reason, all of those things combined comforted me and made me feel safe.

Maddie got off at her house. Like most in Boutin, hers was built on stilts. When you couldn't control the water, you had to outsmart it. The narrow stilts holding up her house were the gray of the sky and almost disappeared into it, making it look like her house was floating. Reed, her little brother, stomped in every puddle on the way up the gravel driveway. Maddie fussed him as the bus pulled away.

The bus was mostly empty by the time we crossed Low-Water Bridge. It was flat and wide open here, past hurricanes having taken the trees and some of the houses. Every once in a while, lonely poles rose out of the ground, reminders of a house that hadn't been rebuilt. Beyond that, it was all marsh grass and canals. And in between the two was home.

The bus stopped at the end of my driveway. I pulled on my hood, gave Ms. Shelby a thumbs-up, and sprinted to the house. There were too many puddles to dodge, and my shoes and socks were soaking wet by the time I made it to the front porch. I shook off like a dog and yanked open the screen door.

Nonnie stepped out of the kitchen. Her pants had been rolled a few times at the ankles, but the edges were still frayed where they dragged on the ground. I'd always wondered how God crammed all of Nonnie's grit and grump into her. Papa had always said Nonnie had a gallon's worth of tough in a pint-sized container. But he'd only said that when he was sure she wasn't listening.

"You look like a drowned possum."

"I am a very hungry drowned possum." And I'd managed to bring a lot of the rain in with me.

Nonnie kissed me and gave me a little push. "Go get out of those wet clothes and come on in the kitchen. I made a gumbo."

Nonnie said I love you with food.

I peeled out of my clothes and tossed them into a soggy mess in the bathtub. I slid on thick socks and sweatpants and a sweatshirt and padded into the kitchen.

Nonnie already had my gumbo on the table.

I filled my spoon, blew on it a few times, and shoveled in several mouthfuls. We'd caught the shrimp and crab ourselves, and Nonnie made her roux extra dark and smoky, just the way I liked it. She'd also been extremely generous with the Tony's—it was salty and spicy and perfect. If home had a taste, it would be my nonnie's seafood gumbo.

The wind blew. Rain splattered against the kitchen window. I shivered.

"Have you heard from Mama?" She worked forty minutes away in Carolton. I wished she didn't have to. I didn't like the fact that she was there when we were here. What if the road went underwater and she was caught on the other side? I didn't want her to have to stay the night in Carolton. I wanted her home.

"I have not."

I tapped my fingers on the table. Reminded myself that this was south Louisiana and Mama drove in the rain all the time. She'd be fine. But it felt like I had my own rainstorm going on inside, and I'd only really feel steady once we were all sitting around the kitchen table.

Nonnie frowned at my antsy fingers and poured herself a cup of coffee. "Have I ever told you about the time I saw the roux-ga-roux?"

"Many times." Other people's grandmas told stories. Mine told yarns.

"Hmph. Then maybe you should tell it to me."

I shook my head. Nobody could weave a tale like Nonnie. She made the impossible seem possible.

"Somebody is going to have to tell the Robichaux stories after I'm gone," she said.

I stared at the scarred table. Papa had built it out of cypress when he and Nonnie had gotten married. They'd eaten all their meals here. Mama had done her homework here. They'd paid bills and played cards and prayed at this table.

Cypress was a soft wood. If I looked really hard, I could see loops and swirls of letters and numbers. Knife marks. Stains. If this table could talk, it would have as many stories as my nonnie.

So she must have really believed in me if she was putting me in charge of the family stories. Not that I couldn't do it. I was a Cajun, like my nonnie, and a Robichaux. It was just that I didn't think I had fully inherited her story magic.

The rain eased up enough that I could hear tires on gravel. I stopped drumming my fingers and took another bite of gumbo. Its warmth filled my belly.

The front door opened. I heard Mama hang up her raincoat, and Nonnie gave me a quick wink as I relaxed back into my chair.

"They closed the office early," Mama said as she came into the kitchen. "Bayou Lafourche is over its banks in some places."

I got up and gave her a quick squeeze. "I'm glad you're home."

She squeezed back. "Me too." She fixed herself a bowl of gumbo and sat at the table with us.

My insides didn't feel so swampy anymore.

"I stopped and got gas on the way home," Mama said, "but I only had the one gas can in the trunk, so it isn't much."

"I don't think we'll need the generator," said Nonnie.

Because this wasn't a hurricane or some kind of major storm. This was just rain.

Until it wasn't.

Chapter Two

It rained all night. When it rained like that, you forgot what the world sounded like when it wasn't raining. It was kind of like having a whole bunch of bees buzzing around in your head. Made it hard to remember what quiet was.

I climbed out of bed and looked out the window. Our driveway had drowned, along with our grass, and the azalea bush by the mailbox was just trying to keep its head above water.

It wasn't doing a very good job. And it was still raining.

I was glad our house was up on stilts.

Mama and Nonnie were both in the kitchen cooking as fast as they could.

"Thirty-one inches of rain in the past forty-eight hours," the radio said.

"Gotta get all this cooked before the power conks out," Nonnie said.

"Have a biscuit," Mama said.

I slathered fig preserves on a biscuit and paced the kitchen while I ate it.

"You're going to wear a hole in that floor," Nonnie told me. She was barefooted and wearing a pair of jeans that had to be older than I was. She had flour on her T-shirt.

I waved my sticky fingers at the mound of food on the stove. "Who's going to eat all this?" I could eat a lot. This was more than that.

"No such thing as too much food," Nonnie said.

It was easier to let Nonnie have the last word sooner. Otherwise she would just wear you down and get the last word later.

I grabbed another biscuit and turned on the news in the living room. Paced as they showed flooding up north in Baton Rouge. Lots of places that never flooded were getting hammered.

I couldn't decide if that made me sad or angry. I decided to be both.

Water is stubborn. It taps a rock until it wears a hole right through it.

Plop.

My science teacher said that was how the Grand Canyon was made.

Plop. Plop.

I looked up. The ceiling was wet. The spot looked a little like Abraham Lincoln.

That bullheaded water had found its way through.

"Mama!"

"What have I told you about hollering at me?"

I knew better than to holler again. I dodged another drip and hurried into the kitchen. "We've sprung a leak."

"What's that?" Nonnie kept her back to me. She was making a roux, which meant she was stirring the flour and oil mixture constantly so that it wouldn't burn. The entire house smelled like roux, a normally comforting smell that meant good food. But right then, I felt anything but comforted.

"It's raining in the living room!"

Mama stopped chopping celery. Nonnie stopped stirring. Then they both jumped forward like they'd been goosed by the devil.

They ran into the living room and tilted their heads back. Nonnie muttered something in Cajun French. I only snagged a word or two, but I understood enough to know better than to repeat it.

"I hope the whole roof doesn't come down on us," Mama said.

"It won't," Nonnie said. "It's one spot. It would take a lot more than that to bring the roof in."

Maybe Nonnie hadn't looked out the window in a while. There was a whole lot going on out there.

Nonnie frowned. "I'm going up there."

"No, I'll go." I chased right behind her.

"I'm not too old to climb those stairs."

"Now don't get your caneçons in a knot," I said, and

she huffed at me. She was most of the way to knotted caneçons already. "It's just easier for me to get up there." The roof sloped and you had to balance on small beams so you wouldn't fall through the ceiling. "My knees just turned thirteen. Yours are—"

"Watch it," she said.

Mama pulled down the stairs, and I stepped around Nonnie. "You stay right here and tell me what to do," I said. "You're good at bossing."

"Like somebody else I know," she grumbled.

Mama handed me a flashlight. "Be careful."

I clambered up the ladder. The rain was even louder up here. My light bounced off cardboard boxes full of Christmas decorations. At least one of them was wet.

"How bad?" Nonnie shouted.

I shone the beam on the ceiling. The wet spot didn't look anything like Abraham Lincoln from here. It looked like a whole heap of trouble. "We need something to catch the water."

"Heads up!" Nonnie tossed two towels up the stairs. "Sop up the water while I get a bucket."

I had to walk hunched over. I soaked up the puddle best I could and threw the wet towels down the stairs. They hit the floor with a splat.

"Coming up!" Nonnie climbed halfway up the stairs and handed me a bucket, which I placed under the drip.

I hoped it would hold.

When I got out of the attic, Mama was throwing

stuff into plastic bins. I packed Nonnie's grandma's quilt. Mama added an old family Bible and some photo albums.

Water didn't care what couldn't be replaced. Water had eaten our yard and nibbled at our house and maybe wanted to snack on our stuff. Water was hungry.

The phone rang in the kitchen. Nonnie answered. Most people in Boutin still had a landline—the cell service was as inconsistent as the weather.

"Oh no, Ida. How bad?"

Mama and I stopped what we were doing and hurried into the kitchen.

"Okay, I'm headed your way." Nonnie hung up the phone. Her mouth was tight, and she had that set to her jaw that meant she was annoyed and worried all at the same time. "I've got to go out."

Mama's eyebrows made it very clear she did not like that. I looked out the window. All I saw was water.

"Ida Labatut's house is taking on water and her car won't start."

Nonnie could give a tongue-lashing that would sting for days, but she'd also give a hungry neighbor the last biscuit in the house. She just wouldn't get all warm and fuzzy about it. We followed her into the living room.

"You're going to need my help," Mama said, grabbing a cap from the peg behind the door and wrestling her hair underneath it. Mama's hair was so brown it was almost black, and all wavy and wild from the humidity.

"To drive the boat?" Nonnie was already digging rain gear out of the hall closet. "Stay here with Jillian."

"You're not leaving me here either," I said. I didn't bother with a cap. My hair was just as unruly as my mama's and twice as long, so there was no way all that mess was going into a cap. But I grabbed a rain jacket. I would not sit in my house while other people needed help. Robichauxs showed up for their neighbors.

Nonnie grumbled in Cajun French and Mama pressed her lips into a thin line and I stepped into Papa's old waders. They were too big.

Everything about today was very big.

"You'll be worried about me the entire time you're out there if you don't let me go."

Five minutes later, we were all tromping down the back steps.

Nonnie had a shrimping boat parked at the marina, but she also had a couple of bateaux out back that we used for frog gigging or fishing in shallow water. Both were parked under the house, and though we normally had to pull them to water, today, they were already floating.

Water crept toward our knees as we went down the stairs. As Nonnie got to the bottom, I suddenly feared the ground wouldn't be there to catch her. I imagined the water would swallow her in one huge gulp.

I held my breath.

But the ground was there, just like always, and she pushed toward the boat.

It was my turn to find the ground, and the cold water lapped at my thighs, but the waders at least kept my pants dry. I flopped over the side of the boat and prayed the bucket in the attic would hold the water until we got back.

We mostly followed the road, though we couldn't see it. Even I could have driven to town with my eyes closed, and Nonnie had lived here a lot longer than I had. We turned right at Mr. Wayne's house. His blue siding was faded and peeling. People didn't build houses for the beauty down here. They were built to be functional, which meant most houses looked the same: squares built high in the air. But with all that water underneath it now, Mr. Wayne's house didn't look as tall as it usually did.

Most of the houses in Boutin, like ours, were on stilts because we got a lot of rain and we were below sea level and the ground was never thirsty enough to drink it all in. The businesses in town were not on stilts. Water lapped at the doors of Dell's Grocery and Louie's Diner and the gas station.

The snowball stand had been pushed off its cinder blocks and sat askew.

My heart felt like it had been knocked sideways too. It wasn't like I hadn't seen floods before. But this wasn't a storm predicted and prepared for, wasn't a hurricane that blew ashore with violent winds and storm surge. This was just a steady rain—that was filling Boutin as if it were a bathtub.

And we couldn't make it stop.

Mrs. Labatut lived on the other side of town, and her house also was not up on stilts. Nonnie pulled right up to where Mrs. Labatut's front porch should have been and grabbed a post.

Mrs. Labatut poked her head out the front door. She was wearing rubber boots and a rain jacket. "Oh good, you brought reinforcements."

"How many bags do you have?" Mama asked.

"Boxes. I have several boxes."

Nonnie gave her a look that would have sent me scurrying to my room, but Mrs. Labatut set her chin and looked almost as stubborn as Nonnie. Nonnie finally sighed and turned the engine off.

Mama tied us to the post and we waded into the house. Water covered the floor and was beginning to creep up the furniture. My heart wanted to slip right between my ribs.

"Back here," Mrs. Labatut shouted.

We found her in what was probably supposed to be a guest room but currently held soggy cardboard boxes. "Grab what you can," she said.

"Ida, don't tell me you called me out here to try and save Eustace's junk."

"It's not junk," Ida argued.

"That's not what you told me six months ago," Nonnie grumbled.

"Eustace spent most of his life collecting pictures of Boutin, and I'm going to save what I can."

"You should have stored this in plastic bins," Nonnie said.

"We should have done a lot of things. Get to carrying." Mrs. Labatut picked up a fairly dry box and hauled it out to the boat.

I eyed the remaining boxes. The ones on the bottom of the stack were soaked through. "What is all this?" I asked.

"Ida's husband was Boutin's self-appointed historian," Nonnie answered.

"What happened to him?"

"He died a few years ago. Ida couldn't bring herself to get rid of this stuff. He's buried not too far from Papa."

He wasn't here to save these pictures, so we would have to do it for him.

Nonnie left with a box in her arms. Mama followed.

Most of the boxes were very heavy. The only one I could lift was wet, but I thought I could make it to the boat. I hugged it to my chest and followed the little ripples left by Mama and Nonnie. It felt good to be moving, doing something, even if this something didn't feel much more than nothing. Being busy kept some of the worry out. Much of Mrs. Labatut's stuff was ruined, and the water was steadily rising.

I only made it to the living room before the bottom fell right out of the box. Black-and-white pictures and yellowed newspaper clippings splashed into the dirty water.

"Oh!" I scooped a handful of pictures off the top of

the stack before they drowned. I shoved them down into my waders, trying to keep them dry. Mrs. Labatut was going to have to replace her carpet and her Sheetrock and her furniture. She couldn't replace these. I managed to get one more handful of pictures tucked away before they were completely submerged.

Mama came back in the door and saw my mess. The pictures were gone and the wrecked box bobbed in the living room water and there was nothing I could do about any of it.

"That's not your fault," Mama said. "We can't salvage it all."

That didn't make me feel one bit better, but Nonnie said the truth didn't always get to be helpful—sometimes the truth was just the truth.

Mama put her arm around me and steered me outside. Nonnie and Mrs. Labatut climbed in the boat soon after. Nonnie carried a plastic trash bag over her shoulder and looked like a disgruntled Santa Claus. Mrs. Labatut wrestled with a suitcase. I held nothing but two handfuls of worry and a heart full of guilt. Nonnie cranked the engine and eased the boat away from the house.

Several boats floated just beyond the church parking lot, which was still dry. Nonnie parked the boat as best she could.

“There’s nothing to tie off to,” Nonnie told me, “so stay with the boat so it doesn’t float away.”

Babysitting the boat was a completely useless chore, but I’d managed to drop the one thing I’d carried, so I figured they didn’t trust me to do much else. I didn’t like the way that felt.

Mama and Nonnie grabbed boxes and waded toward the church. Father Pierre stood at the entrance to the fellowship hall and helped people inside. He held the door open for Mama and Nonnie and waved at me. I waved back.

Mrs. Labatut climbed out of the boat. She slung the trash bag over her shoulder, and I handed the suitcase to her. It felt like she’d packed rocks.

“Do you need help?” I asked.

“I’ve got it, thanks,” she said, smiling. “You know, you are a Landry through and through. You look just like your daddy.”

I wanted to inherit Nonnie’s toughness and Mama’s kindness. I didn’t want anything from my dad—not even his last name.

I got my brown eyes from both of my parents. And maybe I got my height from the Landry side. Maybe, if my dad and I weren’t standing side by side (and we usually weren’t), a person might think I had his small nose and high cheekbones.

They’d be wrong.

“I’m a Robichaux. And Nonnie says I look like her

mother." She said her mama had antsy fingers too, and a wide smile just like mine, and the same bony ankles. I got real busy keeping the boat from slipping away before Mrs. Labatut could decide if I'd been rude. My mama didn't tolerate disrespect. But I didn't think stating a fact could be rude. And the fact was, I was nothing like my dad.

The rain had stopped completely by the time we made it home. The bucket in the attic had held.

"I'm glad that's over," I said, taking off my rain jacket. I didn't think I could handle seeing one more house with water sneaking in the front door. I was grateful mine was dry, and heartsick for those who weren't so lucky.

Mama looked very sad. "I'm afraid it's only the beginning."

"Nora, we need to cook for the church. Father Pierre said they don't have a lot of supplies and that the church will have to be the shelter since the school gym flooded."

"The school flooded?" I took back everything I'd said about math quizzes as a cold trickle of fear slipped down my spine. Like the church, the school was the one constant in Boutin. It was supposed to be untouchable.

I felt like I might float away on a flood of worry, so I clung to certainties instead.

Based on the number of boats floating outside the

church, half the people in Boutin were helping the other half. That was good.

Our house was dry. We were safe. That was also good.

Sometimes when the bad seemed to be in charge, it was important to remember the good you had tucked in your pockets.

Pockets! I'd been so mad at Mrs. Labatut that I'd forgotten to give her the pictures I'd saved. I peeled out of my waders, and the black-and-white pictures scattered across the floor. They were damp, and a couple of them were a little damaged at the edges. I picked them up and carried them to my room, spreading them across the top of my dresser so they could dry out.

I wouldn't fail Mrs. Labatut again.

Faces young and old stared out at me. I wondered who they were, where they'd lived, how many floods they'd seen. A family smiled out at me in one. Was it Mrs. Labatut's? Her husband's? I wondered if any of the people in the picture were still alive—maybe this young face was an old face I knew and just didn't recognize. In another picture, a pretty woman posed in front of Nelda's Diner. I'd forgotten about that place. Nelda's shut down a few years ago, but they had the best milkshakes. One of the pictures had some water damage, and I picked it up. Several men stood on an old wooden dock, smiling, flaunting a line of fish they'd caught. I flipped the picture over. *Cooper's Dock, Boutin, LA, 1932* was scrawled across the back.

I looked more closely at the picture. I'd never heard of Cooper's Dock, and nothing in this picture looked familiar. I'd thought I knew every square inch of Boutin, but this was one place that I'd never been.

I took the picture to Nonnie.

"Who is this?" I handed it to her.

"Where did you get that?" she asked.

"From the box I dropped. I forgot to give it to Mrs. Labatut. I'll give it back when we go to the church."

Mama leaned over Nonnie's shoulder. "I don't know them."

Nonnie flipped the picture over. "1932? How old do you think I am?" She glared at me. Flipped the picture back over.

"What about Cooper's Dock?" I asked.

Nonnie shrugged. "No idea."

A place in Boutin Nonnie didn't know either? Now I had to find out.

For once, I wanted to tell Nonnie a story she'd never heard before.

I went back to my room and put the picture of Cooper's Dock on the dresser with the rest of them. I put on dry clothes, snuggled up with a blanket, and stared out my bedroom window. The water looked dark and much deeper in the fading light.

I was glad to be home.

Chapter Three

Don't forget the coconut cake!" Nonnie shouted from the truck.

I stomped back up the stairs. We'd been trying to leave for the past ten minutes, but it wasn't easy getting everything that Mama and Nonnie had been cooking out of the house. Nonnie's brother Uncle Pete was already down at the church cooking a jambalaya.

Nonnie said if you didn't know how else to help people, feeding them was a good place to start.

And I didn't know how else to help. After we'd lost power, we'd hooked the TV up to the generator long enough to catch the evening news. Louisiana was hurting. Most of the flooding was north of us, in places that normally didn't flood, as levees breached and rivers poured over their banks and into subdivisions. Several groups from Boutin had headed there to help out.

But Nonnie said our community needed all the help we could give, so that's what we were doing.

The pictures were tucked safely in my pocket as we

drove to the church. The water had been going down for the past three days, but it left a whole lot of mess behind. Mud covered the road in spots, and debris gathered by flood waters blocked driveways and ditches. The power had come back on this morning, thank goodness, but it kept flickering like it didn't want us to get too used to it.

All of Boutin looked soggy and sad.

Halfway to town, a wooden barricade blocked the right lane. The road had crumbled away, leaving a gaping hole.

"Wonder how long it'll take them to plug that?" Nonnie muttered as she eased into the left lane. I stared at the puddle of water tough enough to chew through asphalt.

Dell's Grocery was closed, but the doors were propped open and Dell Jr. had a crew hauling out trash. I waved as we passed. Imagined a river of melted ice cream snaking down the freezer aisle. Almost everything in that store had probably gone bad. Poor Mr. Dell.

St. Joseph Catholic Church was the tallest building in town. Most of the parking lot was still underwater, but Uncle Pete had found a dry spot nearby. Nonnie parked behind his truck, blocking him in.

"Uncle Pete's going to fuss you for that," I said.

Nonnie shut off the engine. "I'm not worried about Pete. He might be older, but I'm meaner."

"No argument here," Mama said.

"Jumping Jillie Bean!" Uncle Pete said. He was

wearing a dirty John Deere hat and an enormous smile. He squeezed me when I got close enough to hug. He was soft around the middle, and it was nice to relax into him for a bit.

"Smells good," I told him. Like family get-togethers and Saturday afternoons.

"You don't have to tell me."

Uncle Pete made amazing jambalaya in a town where most people made dang good jambalaya. In south Louisiana, the best cooking was done outside on a burner, with a pot big enough to bathe in and a wooden spoon most Northerners would mistake for an oar.

"Wanda Marie, there's twenty open parking spots over there."

"I'm too old to walk that far."

Uncle Pete narrowed his eyes. "You're only old when it's convenient."

"And today it's convenient." She kissed his cheek. "I made you a coconut cake, you old fart. It's in the back seat."

"Park wherever you want." He gave the jambalaya a good stir. "Lots of hungry folks here. Everyone wanting gossip too." He nodded toward the church. "Maddie's inside with her mama." Uncle Pete was Maddie's grandpa.

I'd find Maddie later—I needed to get these pictures to Mrs. Labatut.

The fellowship hall was full of people milling around

with Styrofoam cups of coffee. Adults used cups of coffee like my cousin Reed used his security blanket—just something warm to hold. Everyone was drier than the last time I was here. I didn't see Mrs. Labatut.

But I did see Mrs. Anderson playing bourré with a group of ladies in the corner of the fellowship hall.

"Hi, Mrs. Anderson," I said.

She looked up from her cards, frowning. "Jillian Robichaux? I'm not buying anything."

"I'm not selling anything," I said. "I was looking for Mrs. Labatut."

"She's gone," Mrs. Anderson said, looking back at her cards and reorganizing them.

"Good thing," Mrs. Domingue said. Flood or no, she was perfectly put together as always in black slacks and a red blouse. Her silver hair shone against her dark skin. She cut her eyes at me. "Ida cheats."

"Where'd she go?" I asked.

"Her son came to get her. She's staying with him in Houston."

"For how long?" A Boutin without Mrs. Labatut felt a little empty. I saw her at Mass every week—she always wore bright lipstick and carried an ugly purse. People practically fought over her chocolate cake at bake sales.

"I feel like I'm being grilled by the FBI," Mrs. Anderson said. "I don't know that she's coming back. Her son has been trying to get her to come live with him awhile. She's got some heart trouble."

And the closest doctor was in Carolton.

I pulled the pictures out of my pocket and showed them to the group. "I wanted to ask her about these."

"What are they?"

"Pictures I saved from her house the other day." I didn't mention how useless I'd felt when the majority of them had sunk beneath the dirty water. "I forgot to give them back. I also wanted to know about the people in the pictures."

Mrs. Domingue waved her hand. "Ida probably wouldn't know anyway—heck, her husband probably didn't even know. He just saved them."

"Eustace was a hoarder," Mrs. Anderson said. "He collected all that junk because no one else wanted it."

For some reason I felt so sad that someone's life, their stories, weren't wanted. We told stories about Papa all the time. It made remembering him easier.

"Have y'all ever heard of Cooper's Dock?" I put that picture on top.

Mrs. Anderson put down her cards and leaned closer. "Well I'll be. That's my grandpa." She tapped one of the men on the end.

That unsettled feeling I'd been toting around turned to hope. Not knowing a place in Boutin had made me feel like a stranger in my hometown, a little bit like a fraud. Maybe Mrs. Anderson would give me a story about Cooper's Dock that I could share with Nonnie. I'd never known a story about Boutin that she hadn't known first.

I showed Mrs. Anderson the back of the picture.

"Where is Cooper's Dock? It says Boutin here, but I've never heard of it."

"That's because it went underwater before any of us were born." She squinted at the picture. "All of that area south did."

"Flood?" I asked.

"You can call it that. Half of the Boutin that was here when my grandfather was young is underwater now."

"What?" Surely Boutin hadn't been twice as big then as it was now. How was that even possible? Towns didn't shrink like sweaters put through the dryer. "Can you tell me about Cooper's Dock?"

She shrugged. "There's nothing to tell. It was a weathered dock on Old Man Cooper's property. It went underwater and didn't resurface, like a lot of things down here. They've been talking about the eroding coast for years now, but Boutin is still here."

"Most of it," Mrs. Domingue muttered.

"What else is gone?" I asked her.

"Too much to remember. Fiddler's Point. Farmland on the east side of town. You can fish where my grandpa used to hunt."

"That old juke joint is gone now," Mrs. Anderson said. "I snuck in there a time or two when I was a teenager."

Mrs. Domingue smiled. "That doesn't surprise me a bit."

My anger started as a spot somewhere around my

belly button, but before I knew it, that anger took up all the space in my chest. It made it hard to breathe. Because they were smiling. And joking. And acting like it was no big deal that entire areas of Boutin just didn't exist anymore.

I needed to know that we'd come back from this flood stronger than ever, that the damage was temporary. I did not want to hear that pieces of my home had been slipping away since before I was born and no one had done anything to stop it.

How could a place just be gone? Home wasn't allowed to desert us.

It hadn't been easy when my parents had first gotten divorced. Every time I missed my dad, or he bailed on our weekends, Nonnie and Papa took me out in the boat. Nonnie would tell me stories, and Papa would tell me the names of trees or birds and teach me to bait my line or throw a net. And every single time I'd felt better.

I didn't like thinking that Boutin was abandoning me too.

I managed to shove that mad into a dark corner long enough to speak. "Do y'all have pictures of any of that?"

"Maybe?"

Mrs. Anderson shook her head. "I doubt someone took a picture of that juke joint. It was ugly. And how were we to know it wouldn't always be there?"

We took pictures of people because we knew they'd change—grow up, get old, move away, die. But we expected places to stay put, to remain when we couldn't, and then they up and disappeared too. I understood then what Eustace Labatut had been doing. He wasn't a hoarder—he was a collector, trying to preserve memories because the real thing was slipping away. I wondered how many places no longer existed and now were completely lost because I'd dropped that blasted box. Now those pictures would sit in the abandoned house until the water receded and they had to be thrown out. I looked at the picture of Cooper's Dock again. *If* the water receded.

Maybe Boutin needed a new collector.

Mrs. Anderson waved me away. "Go on so I can play cards."

Mrs. Domingue looked like she felt a little sorry for me. She winked at me. "She's just mad because I've taken most of her money."

I stacked the pictures into a neat pile and tucked them safely into my pocket before leaving the ladies to their card game.

Maddie was setting a pitcher of sweet tea on a table when I found her. "How's the roof?" she asked.

"Holding. How's your house?"

"Still fine. But I couldn't spend one more minute stuck inside with Reed. He's part feral wolf." She crossed her arms. She looked like a miniature version of her mama when she did that, a tiny constellation of freckles across her nose and hazel eyes that seemed to see not just what things were but what they meant. "So I guess you've heard."

"About?"

"The school."

"Nonnie told me it flooded, but I haven't heard how bad."

Maddie lowered her chin. "Bad."

Right now, everything was bad. "Like out of school for a week?"

"Like out of school for months."

"Months?" We did not take months to get back on track down here. We rolled up our sleeves and got to work. "I'm not repeating seventh grade."

"They're sending us to Carolton Middle."

"What?" No one else in the room seemed to have noticed that the floor had gone wonky. Mrs. Anderson slapped down a card and cackled. Mr. Thibault kept chatting with Father Pierre. But I felt suddenly off-kilter. "For how long?"

"Until they can get the school cleaned and repaired."

How long did it take to mop a floor? Mr. Brooks said he'd have our roof fixed in a week. "Like until Christmas?"

Maddie gave me a pitying look. "If we're lucky."

Carolton was forty minutes away. I didn't know anyone there. And I'd seen their school. It was a lot bigger than ours. Like, I'd-get-lost-on-my-way-to-class big.

"Why can't we go to school here?" There were

Sunday school classrooms and other places we could probably cram into. "Or what about those white metal trailers that other schools have? We could get those."

"Call the superintendent," Maddie suggested. "You and he work out a plan. I'm sure they haven't thought of any of those."

"Don't you get sassy with me, Maddie Louise Richard. Aren't you upset about this?"

Maddie turned to look at me. The humidity made her hair curl in tiny ringlets around her face. "I'm upset about *this*." She spread her arms wide.

Neighbors sleeping on cots instead of their own beds. Friends who had lost some things, or most things, or everything.

I flushed with shame. I was lucky.

"Let's drive out to the school," I told Mama on our way home. I wanted to see the damage for myself. It couldn't be so much that sending us to Carolton was the best option.

"That side of town is still mostly underwater," she said. "The canal came up quick but is taking its time going back down. And Susie was telling me that one part of the roof collapsed." She shook her head at my expression. "It was an old roof."

The entire school was old. My grandparents had

graduated from there. My parents. Aunts and uncles and cousins twice removed.

"It'll be okay," Mama said. "Boutin has survived worse."

I nodded. Robichauxs were resilient. But I thought about all the places the ladies had said were taken by the water, and I didn't feel Robichaux-resilient. I just felt scared.

Nonnie's stories always made me feel safe. I wondered if me telling her one would work too. "Cooper's Dock—"

"Who's parked in my spot?" Nonnie asked as we turned onto the road to our house.

I didn't recognize the truck. Nonnie pulled in behind it and we climbed out.

The truck door opened, and a deep voice told someone left inside the truck to "stay."

I stopped in the middle of our driveway, which was mostly mud and extremely large puddles. Over half the yard remained underwater.

The man turned around. He was tall and broad-shouldered with laugh lines permanently etched around his mouth and eyes. He wasn't smiling now. He just looked nervous.

"Bobby!" my mom said.

"Nora. Wanda." His face relaxed a little bit. "Hey, Jillie Bean."

"Hi, Dad."

Chapter Four

It had been almost a month since my dad had called and more than four months since I'd seen him. He hardly ever came back to Boutin, which was why it was so strange seeing him standing in our front yard.

He held out his arms, and I hesitated for only a moment before giving him a hug. His shirt was soft against my cheek, but I couldn't quite relax into this hug as much as I had Uncle Pete's.

Dad patted my back and stepped away. "I'm glad to see y'all didn't flood."

"You're not coming around to borrow money, are you?" Nonnie asked. Her arms were crossed, and she had the same look on her face as when she found a garfish on the end of her line—like she didn't have any use for what she was looking at.

Mama shot her a sharp glance. Nonnie was very good at ignoring those.

"No, of course not." He waited, but no one said anything. "Um, I need a place to stay."

He hadn't come by just to check on us—he needed something. I wasn't surprised. Seven years ago, Mama had told Dad she needed an equal partner and Dad said he didn't have any more to give. He left Boutin (I wasn't enough to keep him close by), and I saw him on weekends when he wasn't working (which wasn't often since he took a lot of overtime). Maybe at first I'd wanted my parents back together. But now? I probably knew more about Mr. Wayne from down the street than I did about Dad.

"I'm living around Thibodaux now," he said. "Did you know?"

"We knew," Mama said. "You told Jillian that the last time you called. I believe that was a while back now." Mama's voice was polite, but a wide stripe of anger ran smack down the middle. Dad looked like he regretted having to face the Robichaux women. His fingers tapped anxiously against his thigh. I realized with a jolt that mine were doing the same thing. I shoved my hands in my pockets.

"My house flooded. Water nearly up to the kitchen counters. Barely made it out with the truck, and then I spent two nights sleeping in it because the hotels were full and the shelters wouldn't let me in with my dog."

I glanced into the cab of his truck, noticing the golden ball of fur sitting in his passenger seat. He'd never had a dog before because he worked offshore and was gone for weeks at a time. He'd always stressed how very little time he had for anything other than work. I wondered how this dog fit into all that. The dad I knew didn't really like having to be responsible for anyone other than himself.

"I'm willing to pay rent for the couch," he said. "But my house is a total loss. I had three feet of water in there, and it's going to be a while before I can get back in. Please. I need somewhere to sleep." He lowered his voice. "And I just don't have anywhere else to go."

I knew Mama would say yes. She was kind and compassionate and forgiving, and she would not be able to turn him away. I could see the yes in her face.

I wasn't sure how I felt about that.

"You'll have to ask Mom," she said.

Nonnie squinted one eye, like she was trying to figure out the best way to remove him from the property. I saw the hope disappear in Dad's face as swiftly as the blowing out of a candle.

Nonnie jerked her finger at me. "Actually, you have to ask her."

I froze. I liked my life exactly the way it was—the uncertainty of what Dad would do to that quite frankly scared me. But he was my dad, and he needed help. "Sure."

It was what Robichauxs did.

Abandoning those you shouldn't was something my dad might have done.

I wasn't a Landry anymore. When I was in fourth grade I'd gotten detention for disrespect because I'd gotten sassy with my teacher for being forced to write *Jillian Landry* on my papers.

"I'm a Robichaux!" I'd argued.

"Your legal name is Landry, and that's what I have to go by."

I'd wanted my name to match my family's, so Mama had approached Dad about the change. He'd refused at first, but he eventually agreed, I suspect after a lengthy phone call from Nonnie.

So even though I knew it was going to be awkward having Dad in the house, I agreed, if for no other reason than to show him I was a Robichaux, not a Landry. Robichauxs lived in Boutin—Landrys moved away—and Robichauxs put family first.

The tension went out of Dad's shoulders at my answer, and he smiled at me. "It's just temporary, I promise."

"You dang right it's only temporary," Nonnie grumbled, and she went inside.

I helped Mama pull out sheets and blankets and stack them on the sofa while my dad unloaded his truck. He didn't have much, just a few boxes he stashed outside in the shed and a couple of Walmart bags with a change of clothes and some shampoo. I watched through the window as he crossed the yard a couple of times, his dog less a shadow and more a golden ball of light following him around.

"Lucy won't be any trouble," Dad promised as he

came into the living room. I couldn't remember the last time he'd stood in this room. The golden retriever followed him in.

"If she pees in this house, you're both sleeping outside," Nonnie shouted from the kitchen.

But Lucy looked like a very good girl. She was a big dog, but she was calm—no bouncing or barking or knocking things over. Her blond hair was long and a little wavy, and her ears flopped forward. A tiny tuft of hair stood straight up on the top of her head, and something about the shape of her mouth made it look like she was smiling. She sniffed Mama, who patted her head, then stuck her cold nose in my hand.

"She won't hurt you," Dad said, smiling.

Lucy sat next to me and nudged my hand again. I scratched behind her ear, and her tail thumped against the floor.

Dogs always seemed to have a little happiness stored away. And they didn't mind sharing.

Lucy got up and padded back over to Dad, pawing his leg until he squatted down and rubbed both of her ears. She leaned on him.

That was something I'd never really been able to do.

"Since when do you have a dog?" I asked. He'd always been too busy for dogs or daughters.

"Since about four months ago. My new job means I'm home every night now. I got tired of coming home to an empty house."

I'd never even seen his new place. I told myself that it wasn't hurt that I felt as I looked at the dog's trusting face—because that would be stupid.

"She limped into my yard one night. Something had gotten after her. She needed me." He leaned his fore-head against the dog's and scratched the side of her neck. "We needed each other."

I swallowed the lump in my throat. Maybe *we* had needed him. But no, I didn't really believe that. Mama and I had always had each other, had Nonnie and Papa, had extended family and an entire community right here if we'd needed them.

"We'll let you get settled." Mama put her arm around me and steered me into the kitchen. "You okay?"

I refused to be jealous of a dog. Besides, after Dad left, Mama and I had moved in with Nonnie and Papa. And I'd come home every night to people who loved me and he went home to an empty house and no one to blame but himself. "Are you?"

"The only way he can upset me these days is to upset you." She clasped her hands tight and looked toward the living room. "I sure do hate he's going through this."

My mama had the kindest heart. Right now mine seemed awfully small in comparison.

"Get to helping," Nonnie said. We'd managed to eat or give away most of the food we'd cooked. She tossed me the potato peeler.

Sometimes if I got real busy with one thing, I forgot

to be so busy with what Nonnie called my simmering and stewing.

"The entire cemetery is underwater again," Nonnie said. She was flitting between three different pots.

Mama started chopping onions. "I figured."

The cemetery went completely underwater every time it flooded, but it was mostly underwater all the time now. I didn't like thinking about Papa out there. I wanted to remember him with a fishing pole in his hand or helping me catch fireflies in the backyard.

"I figured we'd go out on All Saints', clean it up a bit. The water should be gone by then," Nonnie said.

"One can hope." But Mama didn't sound so sure.

Nonnie gave me a wicked grin. "Mary Delapasse wants her sister Agnes declared a saint."

I could feel my worry begin to settle to the bottom at the promise of a Nonnie story.

"This is Agnes Rivault who got kicked out of Dell's Grocery for cussing him?" I asked.

"The same."

"Surely that wasn't the miracle," Mama said. "I'm fairly certain Nonnie has cussed Dell too, and she's hardly a saint."

I grinned. Nonnie said my neck disappeared when I was upset, just like a turtle's. My shoulders hitched up around my ears. But Mama's and Nonnie's voices helped, and I felt my shoulders go back to where they were supposed to be.

Nonnie cut her eyes at Mama in a warning. "Mary cut her foot on a rusty nail and it got infected. She stuck it in the water next to Agnes's headstone."

I pointed the potato peeler at Nonnie. "And you're telling me that the nasty water, with God only knows what floating in it, healed her foot?"

"No," Nonnie said. "I'm here to tell you that her sister Agnes healed her. And Mary's son will swear to it. Mary's taking everyone she knows with any kind of ailment, from heart trouble to hangnail, out to bathe in that water."

Mama snorted. I caught sight of Nonnie's face and giggled. Mama and I laughed harder then, hard enough that we both had to stop what we were doing just to hold ourselves up. Tears rolled down my cheeks, and I wasn't sure if all of them were from laughing. My stomach ached, but in that good way, how laughter somehow fills you up and empties you out all at the same time.

We stopped laughing when Dad walked in the kitchen. Mama took a deep breath. I swiped at my face.

"Let me help," he said. "Got to earn my keep." Dad gave us an uncomfortable grin. "I wouldn't want to get on the wrong side of the Robichaux women."

It was Nonnie's turn to laugh. "Bobby," she said when she finally got ahold of herself, "it's a dang sight late for that."

Mama hid her laugh in a cough. Dad rubbed the back of his neck, which had turned red. Lucy peeked into the kitchen, her head lowered in uncertainty but fluffy tail wagging hopefully.

"No dogs in the kitchen!" Nonnie snapped.

"Jillian, would you mind taking Lucy out while I do this? Her leash is on top of my stuff."

Lucy's ears perked up at the word *out*. So did mine. The kitchen felt smaller with him in it.

I found the leash in the living room. Lucy swung her head side to side, prancing back and forth on her front feet.

"Do you want to go outside?" I asked. I grudgingly felt a little grateful to Lucy for giving me an excuse to escape.

She pranced faster, still swinging her head. I clipped the leash to her collar. She danced to the door.

I took her to the high spots in the yard. There weren't many. "You better not be picky where you potty." She sniffed every spot twice.

We walked around the side of the house. The kitchen was all lit up, and Dad stood at the sink, his forehead creased with worry.

Lucy sat down beside me and leaned her head against my knee. My chest felt all tight and itchy as I looked at her sweet face, and I waited a beat before reaching down and patting her. Nothing my dad did was her fault. But I knew better than to get attached to Lucy. She was Dad's dog, and Dad never stayed long.

Chapter Five

I was already awake when Mama tiptoed into my room. I'd been that way for a while.

"Good morning," Mama whispered. She sat on the edge of my bed. "You ready?"

I was ready to get out of this house. Mama and Nonnie and Dad and I had been bumping into each other all week. I was ready to see my friends again, for my school to be back to normal. I was not ready to be a new student at a new school. I wanted to tell Mama that I was scared.

But my mama wasn't afraid of anything, so I ignored the way my stomach was twisting around on itself, like I'd eaten a fistful of snakes. I pretended to be Robichaux-brave.

"I'm ready." And because it was dark, Mama believed me.

"Good. Because I'm making my famous French toast this morning."

That did make me feel a little better. Mama dipped

the bread in pancake batter instead of just egg and milk and it was basically the best breakfast in the whole world.

By the time I was dressed, Mama had my stack of French toast on the table. If Mama had made anything else, I might have been too nervous to eat. But there was no way I was letting this go to waste.

"You're going to spill my coffee," Nonnie said.

I realized I was bouncing my leg up and down hard enough to shake the table.

"Sorry." I made my legs go still, but it wasn't easy to keep them that way.

"Did I ever tell you about your mom's first day of high school?" She tried to keep her face innocent, but the corner of her mouth twitched. She took a sip of her coffee to hide it and looked at me over the rim of her cup. Her eyes had that mischievous glint they sometimes got when she was about to do something she knew she probably shouldn't. Mama's eyebrows went all pointy, which meant someone was in trouble. I knew right then it was going to be a very good story. "No."

"I was probably saving it. But now seems like the perfect time."

"You think breakfast is the perfect time?" Mama asked.

That meant it was probably gross. I no longer had to force myself to be still. All my knots and tangles began to loosen, and I didn't want to be anywhere but at this table for this story. I took another bite of French toast.

"It begins with biscuits and gravy," Nonnie said.

Dad stepped into the kitchen. "Something smells good in here."

Nonnie stopped talking. I huffed.

"Sorry," he said, the tips of his ears pink. "I didn't mean to interrupt."

"Nonsense." Mama aimed that pointy eyebrow at me this time. I got real busy with my breakfast.

"First day at Carolton?" Dad asked.

I chewed and nodded.

"I can give you a ride to school if you'd like."

"Mama's taking me."

"Oh."

Lucy peeked around the door and into the kitchen. Nonnie didn't need to put on her pointy eyebrows. She wore her gruff face two thirds of the day, and it was always in place until her second cup of coffee. Lucy eased back into the living room.

Smart dog.

"When do you go to work?" Nonnie asked Dad.

"Not until tomorrow, technically," he said. "But I'm going to drive out that way this afternoon so they can show me around, get me settled into my temporary spot." Nonnie seemed relieved she wouldn't have to spend the day alone with Dad.

"I could pick you up after school," he told me.

After school I would have to ride the bus because Mama didn't get off work until five thirty. It was what I was used to anyway. I rode the bus home every day after school. I was nervous enough already about going to Carolton. I needed the certainty that at the end of the day I would be going home with the Boutin kids. I wasn't so sure I wanted to be stuck in the truck with my dad for forty minutes either. I had no idea what we would talk about.

"I think I'd rather ride the bus with Maddie."

Dad's jaw tightened, and I tried to ignore my guilt. "Okay. Yeah, I understand that." He forced a smile and took a bite of his breakfast. "Nora, I'd forgotten how good your French toast is."

It wasn't fully daylight when Mama and I pulled out of the driveway, but we weren't the first ones up. People in Boutin worked hard and started early because that was the only way to do it. Mr. Truong was pulling out of his driveway when we passed, and I waved. His daughter was a year below me in school. Mr. Truong's dad had come over from Vietnam, and they'd been shrimpers their whole lives, until the price of gas went up and the price of shrimp went down and Mr. Truong had to take a job in Carolton, like my mom. We passed boats on their way to the launch, hoping for a good day on the water, but mostly we passed cars on their way north, people having to work outside Boutin just to make a living. Nobody wore suits in Boutin. Most people came home dirty, everyone came home tired, and watching the sunset from the backyard mostly made it worth it.

We drove past trash piled on the side of the road, ruined furniture and carpets and cabinets, soggy mountains that got taller every day. It looked like the world's worst yard sale.

Fishing boats lined the canal on the right side of the road. There was always a lot of water between Boutin and Carolton, but there was even more today. Carolton also had piles of debris on the sides of their roads. Maybe their church had a shelter too. Their school, however, had stayed dry while ours hadn't. I couldn't think about how unfair that was since nothing about the flood had been fair.

"Change isn't always bad," Mama said. "I know you aren't excited about Carolton Middle, but instead of thinking that you have to go, think that you get to go. Enjoy the new a little bit. Meet new friends. Learn from new experiences."

My brain knew Mama was right, but it failed to pass along that information to the rest of me. The rest of me still thought we were worried.

"It's only for a little while," I said.

"You'll be complaining about Boutin Middle before you know it."

Carolton Middle was surrounded by planned neighborhoods. Boutin didn't look planned at all. Most of us lived in trailers or old houses up on stilts. In Boutin you learned the value of things, learned to appreciate what you had and fix it when it broke instead of throwing it out completely.

Mama stopped in front of the school. "Everything will be okay." She reached over and squeezed my hand. "Have a great day."

The school was bigger than ours. And newer. A teacher waved me inside. There were kids everywhere. I didn't know if any of them had ever had their lunch stolen in third grade. They didn't know that Maddie was the smartest person in our grade or that I'd won the fourth-grade spelling bee or that you could only believe about half of what Derek said. The unfamiliarity of it all was not a comforting feeling.

Maddie stepped out of a huddle of Boutin students. "Over here."

At home, the grades didn't mix much. But here, the familiar face was better than the stranger, and sixth, seventh, and eighth graders crowded together. Some looked as nervous as I felt. A few, like Derek, tried to look tough.

"Did y'all hear about Katelyn?" Adam asked as we walked up.

We hadn't.

"Gone," Adam told us. "Packed up and moved north, somewhere around Alexandria, I think. She has an aunt there or something."

"Just until they get their house fixed, or forever?" Maddie asked.

"For good. Her mom said she wasn't going to ride out one more flood."

Most of the Carolton kids stared at us. Some looked curious, others like they felt sorry for us. A couple were laughing, and I caught some boy sneering about white rubber boots and fish guts.

A lot of our parents were shrimpers and fishermen and wore white rubber boots. But the insult was stupid because a lot of theirs did too. It wasn't a secret that plenty of Carolton kids thought we were trashy.

I lowered my shoulders (they'd found their way to my ears again) and held up my head. I was proud of being from Boutin.

"Good morning!"

There was a face I recognized. "Mrs. Fontenot!" I said. "What are you doing here?"

"Somebody has to teach y'all English." She smiled. "Doing okay?"

"Fine." Better now. If we had all our same teachers, it wasn't going to be nearly as bad as I'd feared.

"I'm assuming we're having classes in the trailers outside?" Maddie asked. "With all our regular teachers?"

"I hope Mrs. Hebert isn't planning on giving us our math quiz today," I said.

Mrs. Fontenot stopped smiling. "Mrs. Hebert's house flooded. She's gone to Baton Rouge to stay with her daughter."

Boutin was emptying out faster than a cooler of beer at a crawfish boil.

"Is she coming back?" Maddie asked.

"She's teaching algebra at a school there."

She'd taught my mom and dad, taught at Boutin Middle her entire career, and now she was in a strange building in a strange town with students whose families she didn't even know.

The intercom came on, and the hallways stilled. "Welcome back, Panthers, and happy Monday! On the bell, all CMS students will report to their regular first periods. And we would like to extend a warm Panther welcome to all students from Boutin Middle. When the bell rings, please report to the gym to get your schedules. Students and teachers will be in the halls to show you exactly where that is. Have a great day!" The intercom went off with a click, and the bell rang.

The Carolton students scattered, leaving us in a loose huddle in the hall. "Keep up!" Mrs. Fontenot shouted, and she took off. Someone bumped into me and quickly offered an apology without stopping.

More students joined at the intersection. I lost Maddie and the rest of the Boutin crew, though I was pretty sure I could see the top of Maddie's head bobbing along at the front of the crowd. I felt very battered about in the sea of students. Our halls were never this crowded.

Students peeled off into classrooms. I didn't see a single familiar face. Mrs. Hebert wasn't pointing her crooked finger at students running in the halls. Mr. Baker wasn't clinging to his enormous mug of coffee. I followed a line of backpacks left down a hallway. I didn't see a sign for the gym, but I saw daylight, so I took a right.

And found myself standing back outside in a courtyard.

My skin felt hot all over, and I imagined it bright red, this ridiculous beacon that singled me out.

I wanted to go home.

"You lost?"

I turned around to find a girl walking toward me. She was short and Black and wore rainbow-colored tennis shoes.

"No."

The girl didn't know me, or my family, or their stories. I was just a strange face standing in her place—someone who didn't belong. And I was embarrassed to admit I was lost, that the first thing she would know about me was that I couldn't find my way to the gym.

She raised her eyebrows. "So you meant to be standing out here alone in the courtyard?"

Where I was meant to be was at my school in my town.

When I didn't answer, she tried again. "You must be from Boutin."

"I speak English." The words just fell out of my mouth.

"Yeah." She said it slowly, obviously unsure what I was even talking about.

"I mean, the stereotype is that we only speak Cajun

French, but we don't." I don't. And I sort of hated it. I wished I'd been taught like the older people in my family. But it had mostly faded away years ago, when the older generations had been forced to speak English at school and were punished if they didn't.

"You are, like, forty-five minutes from home. We are from the same area."

It felt like I was so much farther away. I blushed. Why was I acting so weird, like I was in some whole other state? I was raw and exposed and very near tears. And making absolutely no sense.

"Want me to show you the gym?"

I didn't know why she was being so nice to me, but I was grateful. I wasn't going to be at Carolton long enough to make friends, but I did appreciate the fact that she was going to be late for class because the strange girl she was trying to help was acting an absolute fool.

I nodded.

"You probably took a left when you were supposed to stay right. I'm headed that way. I'll show you."

I followed her inside.

"I got lost four times my first week here last year," she said. "It can be confusing."

"Our school is too small to get lost in," I said. "Plus, it's a square, so you can't take a wrong turn." Now she probably thought people from Boutin were navigationally challenged. Stick me in the marsh and I could find my way out. But concrete looked all the same to me.

"It's right through there," the girl said, pointing to a set of double wooden doors.

"Thanks."

"I'm Mina."

"Jillian."

Mina smiled. "Welcome!" And then she turned and sprinted down the hall to class.

The Boutin students sat together in the bleachers. I slipped next to Maddie, who shot me a worried look that I ignored.

The Carolton principal walked out onto the court with our Mrs. Melancon.

"I'm glad to see you're on your best behavior," Mrs. Melancon said. She had a wilted look about her, quite different from her usual stern and starched self.

"We'll make you proud, Mrs. M!" Toby Thibault called out. Nervous laughter rippled through the crowd.

"I'm sure you will. This is Mr. Saucier, principal here. I'm sure we're all grateful for his generosity and hard work in making it possible for us to attend CMS."

This was not how I'd imagined seventh grade would be.

"We're glad to have you here," Mr. Saucier said. "Let's get your schedules sorted out."

And for the first time, Maddie and I didn't have every single class together. At least we both had science first period.

We left the gym as a group, but we slowly split up to

find our classes. I got to room 115 first and yanked open the door. I'd forgotten that we'd been in the assembly for a while, that class had been in session that whole time. I froze in horror as every head swiveled to stare at me. At this point in the day, my skin had flushed so often I was afraid I might spontaneously combust. That would be a story to rival Mama's first day. "S-sorry," I managed to stammer as Maddie and Derek came into the room behind me.

The teacher smiled at us. "No problem. Welcome to science!" She sounded awfully excited so early in the morning. Several students rolled their eyes. She glanced down at her roll. "Jillian Robichaux."

My words had gotten all clogged up in my throat, so I just raised my hand a little.

"So you're Maddie."

"Yes, ma'am."

"Welcome. And Derek." She made marks on her paper. "Great. There are three seats in the back. We move around a lot in here, so don't worry. You'll be in the front soon enough. Here are copies of the syllabus I gave each of these students at the beginning of the year." She handed us the stapled papers and let us take our seats. There were plenty of stares. The girl I'd met earlier, Mina, gave me a little wave, but I couldn't even manage a smile. All of Mama's French toast seemed to want to make an appearance. I did not want to be known as the girl who puked. "We were just discussing the flood, and how it fits right into what we're studying in this class."

How lucky for them that the destruction of our school fit so nicely into their science unit. It was one thing to learn about something—it was quite different to actually live it.

"Science is about understanding the world around us, which I feel, of course, is the most important thing we can know and learn about."

Did she understand my world? I kind of doubted it. And what good was learning about pointless science stuff? Until I'd found those pictures, no one had told me that Boutin was half the size it used to be. That was what people needed to be talking about.

"We usually don't get to the biodiversity unit until after Christmas, but considering what just happened here, I've rearranged some things, so we're going to watch this video on the Caminada Project, which was completed not too far from here. Who knows what it is?"

Nobody raised their hand.

"That's sort of what I figured, though I thought maybe those of you from Boutin might. The Caminada Project is practically in your backyard."

What did she know about my backyard? She wasn't from Boutin, and she didn't get to tell me what I should know about. I knew shrimp season and the way the wind shifted right before a big storm and the mess left behind after a flood.

I folded my arms and slouched down in my seat.

The Caminada Headland is Louisiana's largest ecosystem project. It is thirteen miles of restored beach that will protect from storms and provide a place for local and migrating birds.

I thought about Cooper's Dock. How much dirt would have kept it standing? The half of Boutin that Mrs. Anderson said was underwater now—if people had been paying attention, if they'd been willing to work, could it have been saved?

Building the beach cost 216 million dollars.

But Boutin couldn't afford that. We couldn't even afford a traffic light, not that we really needed one—though Mrs. Pitre did have a tendency to run stop signs.

The video ended and Ms. Wilson flipped the lights back on. I blinked and looked around. Mina was doodling in her notebook. Two boys had fallen asleep. But I was leaning forward in my desk.

"This is happening in our state."

Ida Labatut's pictures had opened my eyes to that.

"We are losing land."

We. It wasn't just Boutin—other places were falling away too.

"But we are working to put it back. That's what I hope you learn this year. We live in a delicate balance with nature, and we need to make sure we don't tip that balance. You may feel powerless, but you aren't. One single voice, one small act, can have an impact."

I wanted to stop what was happening in Boutin. I just didn't know how.

Maybe Ms. Wilson wasn't completely awful. Maybe she did know a little bit about what was going on, even if she didn't live there. At least she was talking about it.

But the sliver of hope I felt after class didn't last long. I got lost twice before lunch, then sat in spilled milk in the cafeteria and got teased by some burly boy for having "peed" my pants. When the bell rang at the end of the day, all I wanted to do was get home. I was going to talk Nonnie into taking me fishing before dinner. I needed time on the water.

I didn't have to talk Nonnie into anything. She knew me better than anyone and was standing on the front porch when the bus dropped me off.

"Want to ride out to the cemetery?"

I climbed the porch steps. "Thinking of asking Agnes Rivault for some healing?"

Nonnie waved her hand at the idea. "I'm too ornery to get sick."

"You might be right about that."

"Honey, I'm right about most things." She gave me a little push toward the house. "We'll have to hurry if we want to beat the dark."

I changed clothes and met Nonnie in the living room. Lucy, who was lying on an old blanket on the floor, looked up at me and Nonnie with a plea in her eyes. It was a sad, lonely look, which Nonnie answered with a glare. Lucy put her head on her paws and heaved a pitiful sigh.

Dad was working and had left Lucy alone—a situation I understood. I found myself feeling sorry for her. "Think she can go with us?"

Nonnie rolled her eyes and grumbled under her breath. "Hope she doesn't get seasick."

We'd have to take the boat. We couldn't get to the cemetery in the truck anymore.

Apparently Lucy spoke Nonnie, because the next thing I knew, the dog was prancing toward the door, eyes on her leash. Her tail raked Nonnie's newspaper and sent it fluttering to the floor.

"Dog's got an alligator tail," Nonnie said, but she didn't look all that cranky about it.

Fifteen minutes later, we were in the boat. Lucy had been a bit uncertain at first, but after I got in and showed her it was safe, she followed. She even let me put an orange life vest around her neck.

My body uncoiled as we pulled away from the bank. There were fewer complications out here. No uncertainty. No feeling trapped. My lungs felt like they could hold so much more air, and my worries felt smaller in all this space. I felt smaller too, but not helpless—more like a part of something bigger and better. Being out here knit together the tiny frays in my soul.

Lucy's ears flapped in the breeze. Nonnie steered the boat around a small bend in the canal and avoided the neon flags marking pipelines. "I remember when you couldn't even get a boat through here. This trainasse was no more than a ditch." She pursed her lips and shook her head.

This echoed what Mrs. Anderson and Mrs. Domingue had said, what I'd heard in science today, but why exactly was this canal getting larger? "What happened?"

"Same thing that happened to most of the natural gas pipelines they put in. The water ate at the banks until the ditch got wide enough for a boat. Then two."

I'd spent my whole life on this water, shrimping and fishing and learning the bayous like other people knew their neighborhood streets. Because they had been my neighborhood streets.

But after hearing about the Caminada Project from Ms. Wilson, I was realizing there was still plenty I didn't know.

And I wanted to know.

The outer edge of the cemetery came into view, the fence posts poking up from the water. A dark line on the trees showed how high the water had gotten. It was going down, but not fast enough. Nonnie killed the engine, and the sound of frogs filled the air. A large frog plopped into the water right next to the boat, and Lucy jerked her head toward the sound.

"Don't even think about it," I told her. I could tell by how alert she was that Lucy was definitely still thinking about it, but she thankfully stayed in the boat.

Papa was buried aboveground like most people down here. But the water seemed to have taken that as a challenge. The graves to the left of Papa's were almost completely underwater. His was still visible, but only just.

"I don't want him to go underwater," I whispered. Without thinking, I reached out and put my hand on Lucy's side. Her soft fur was comforting somehow.

Nonnie leaned forward. "That's exactly where he'd want to be. This bayou ran through his veins every bit as much as blood."

I watched the water lap against the graves. More than likely, Nonnie was right. Half of them probably said *Rest in Peace*, and nowhere was more peaceful than this.

We sat in silence for a minute and paid our respects to Papa—even Lucy. She sat still and silent next to me, head tipped back to catch the breeze. I did the same.

Grandpas shouldn't die. Towns shouldn't flood. And home should always be the place where you don't have to worry.

"How was your first day?" Nonnie asked after a bit.

I filled her in. My accidental detours at school today seemed funny anecdotes rather than embarrassing gaffs now that I was outside, my ears filled with frogs and water and wind instead of bells and voices and noise. Lucy seemed to be listening too. She cocked her head and watched as I talked about Ms. Wilson and the Caminada Project.

"I want to show you something," Nonnie said after I'd finished.

She started the boat and steered it down another canal, killing the engine a little while later. "This used to be Boutin's cemetery." The only things visible were a few bricks and corners. "It went underwater probably fifty years ago."

"Fifty?" If I had learned this a week ago I might have been shocked. But after hearing about Cooper's Dock and the Caminada Project, I wasn't as surprised as I might have been.

But fifty years seemed a long time to watch a town go underwater and do nothing.

"It was a pretty big cemetery back in the day. When my mama was young, the town had picnics out here on All Saints' Day, spent the day cleaning and sometimes repainting the graves. Some of the first Robichauxs to settle here are under this water."

"Is this Old Cemetery?"

"It is."

I'd heard people talking about Old Cemetery most of my life. It was supposed to be good fishing. When the old-timers talked about the stones giving the fish places to hide, I'd thought they'd meant rocks and sunken trees and maybe old boats. I'd never realized they meant actual graves. And out of all the fishing spots Papa and Nonnie had taken me, I realized now why we'd never been here. They would have thought it disrespectful.

"Tell me about them." I didn't know these Robichauxs. If I was going to be in charge of our stories, I needed these as well.

"I probably already have. But you know what? I'm not even sure who is buried here." Their names were washed away. These Robichauxs had been lost to the water long before I was born. It took their names, their stories, just like it had taken the land.

I wrapped my arms around myself. I didn't like that thought at all.

"We'd better get home before dark." Nonnie pushed down on the throttle and pointed us toward home.

Chapter Six

After school on a Friday, I found Nonnie sitting on the back porch with a net spread across her lap, gnarled hands repairing small tears.

I sat on the top step, legs in the sun. Lucy dropped a tennis ball next to me. "Go down in the yard first," I told her. The last time we'd played this game, she'd nearly killed herself racing down the stairs. She bounced on her feet, then pawed my leg. "Go down in the yard," I told her.

"Allons, tête dur," Nonnie said.

Lucy looked at us both, then went down the stairs, stopping on the last one to give me a look of exasperation. I laughed and tossed the ball.

"She'll do that until your arm falls off," Nonnie said.

But I didn't mind so much.

"So Millie Lemoine just got out of the hospital," Nonnie said. "She broke both her arm and leg last week."

"How did she do that?"

Nonnie huffed. "Cleaning out her gutters. She's seventy-five years old if she's a day."

"At what age do you get too old to do things?" I asked her. Nonnie had just hauled up several traps from the bayou the day before.

"You hush your mouth," she said. "Your mama and I are planning on running by there tomorrow to take her some groceries and do a few things around her house. Want to come?"

Maybe most kids my age wouldn't want to spend a Saturday doing chores or hanging out with old people. But I liked Millie Lemoine. What I didn't like was feeling useless, which was mostly what I'd been feeling for the past couple of weeks. I couldn't do anything about the flooding or the school. But I could help tomorrow, even if only in small ways. It was something.

"I'm in."

Mama stuck her head out the back door an hour later. I was lying in the grass with my head resting on Lucy, who had finally worn herself out. My head moved up and down as she breathed. It was the stillest I'd been in a while.

Mama held up two huge brown paper bags. Grease soaked through the bottom of one of them. "Junk food." She paused for effect. "And poker night."

The last time we'd played poker Mama had won all our money and then tap-danced across the kitchen shouting *Cha-ching!*

"If I remember correctly, y'all play dirty," Dad said, stepping onto the porch. My head fell to the grass with a *thwap* as Lucy jumped to her feet and raced to Dad's side.

"We do not." Nonnie swelled up indignantly. "We don't spare feelings. It's absolutely not the same thing. Are you afraid we'll take all your money?"

Dad grinned. "Just remember you brought this humiliation on yourself."

Mama kept several jars of change in the laundry room, community money for whoever needed to wash their car or buy a Coke. On poker night, it was shared evenly at the beginning, but the winner kept the money at the end of the night, and we started the fund all over again come washing day.

We spread the junk food across the kitchen counter and filled our plates. Mama had brought home cheese fries and onion rings, boudin balls and smoked sausage. It was my favorite kind of dinner: irreverent finger foods.

Several hands in and I hadn't won yet. This go-around I only had a pair of eights, but I was determined to bluff my way into a little money. Papa had taught me to play poker when I was nine and we were stuck in the house for a couple of days during a tropical storm. But it was

Nonnie who'd taught me to bluff. I tossed in two quarters. "I'm in, and I raise a quarter."

Dad frowned, and Mama examined me rather than her cards. Lucy lay across the threshold to the kitchen, her head on her paws and her tail in the living room. Nonnie eyed her but didn't fuss, since technically Lucy wasn't in the kitchen. Lucy's eyes traveled back and forth between all of us. Maybe she could feel the tension too. We still hadn't figured out how to live together. Dad didn't mean to, but he kept stomping through our rituals, unaware of the steps and not used to the tune.

"So Derek snuck a raccoon into his house last week," I said, hoping to settle the room with a story. He'd caught the thing in his backyard and told us the story yesterday at lunch. "But in the middle of the night it escaped the cardboard box he was keeping it in and pooped all over the house. His dad heard a noise, thought someone was breaking in, and stepped barefooted in the poop. He slid all the way down the hall and was covered in the mess. Derek's grounded now, of course. He said it took a couple of hours to get the floor cleaned."

"Lord, I bet his mama is fit to be tied," my mama said.

"I'd be more worried about his grandma." Nonnie couldn't suppress her grin.

"Didn't she die last year?" I asked.

"Honey, that kind of news travels even to the afterlife."

Dad's entire body shook with laughter. Mama joined

in. Then we were all laughing. Mama snorted and we laughed even harder.

I couldn't remember the last time all four of us had laughed together like that. Maybe never. Most of my worry slipped between the spaces in our laughter.

Stories had a way of healing broken places.

Nonnie put her cards down once she'd recovered. "I fold."

"Me too," said Dad.

"I'm out," added Mama.

And just like that, I won a pile of money with a pair of lousy eights.

"I'd forgotten what this was like," Dad said as he and I both went back for more cheese fries.

"Losing at poker?" I slipped Lucy two fries. She took them gently and retreated to the living room before Nonnie noticed.

"Family." He said the word like a prayer—quiet, careful, hopeful.

I gave him a small smile and the last boudin ball.

Plates full, we sat back down. Dad dealt the next round. "I heard the Shrimp Shed is closing," he said, tossing a card my way.

"What?"

The Shrimp Shed had been here since before Nonnie

was born. People always needed to sell shrimp and gather to spin a tale. Where would all those stories go now?

I imagined them floating on a breeze, lonely like, no one around to hear them.

"When?" Nonnie asked. Her wrinkles looked a lot deeper now that she wasn't laughing.

Mama kept quiet and tried to stare a hole through Dad. That meant she already knew. Poker night must have been her idea of a distraction. I laid my cards down. All the fun had gone right out of the game.

"Not sure when," Dad said, "but Willie told me they'd been struggling to bring in business anyway. Fewer people, fewer boats."

"I used to peel shrimp down there for pocket money," Mama said.

"Me too," Nonnie said. "The school turned into a ghost town during shrimp season. If you weren't on a boat catching shrimp, you were down at the Shed peeling them."

"Hard on your hands," Mama said. "They'd be shredded and sore after a single day, and then we'd go back again."

"But it was worth it when the piggy bank was full," Nonnie said. "Not that mine ever stayed that way."

"What in the world did you spend it on?" I asked. Boutin had never been known for its shopping.

Nonnie laughed. "We had stuff back then," she said. "I bought records and cold drinks and ribbons for my hair."

It was hard to imagine Nonnie with ribbons anywhere.

"But why are they closing?" I asked.

"Well, with the bridges being condemned . . . ," Dad said, then trailed off at the look Mama gave him.

"What bridges?" I asked.

"They aren't condemned," Mama said.

"Yet," Dad added.

"Somebody better tell me what is going on."

Nonnie spoke up. "Nothing is going on. Some kid in a suit from the state has said they aren't going to repair a couple of the bridges and roads here because they didn't get the money from the oil companies that they were supposed to." She rolled her eyes. "No surprise there. I'm surprised more people believed the promises from the state—or the oil companies, considering their pipelines are a huge part of the problem."

"Which bridges?" I asked.

"Collier's and Low-Water." Mama's voice was quiet.

The one to the school. The one to our house.

"How can they do that?"

"They have to use the money for places that matter," Dad said.

"We matter!" I mattered. Home mattered.

"Places with more people," Mama said.

"So the state thinks Boutin is too small to waste money on?"

That made it sound like the people here were too small to worry about. I had enough mad in me that I thought it might burst right through my skin. Instead, it jump-started my legs, which went to bouncing.

"So what does that mean?" I asked.

"Nothing," Nonnie said. But Mama's face didn't look like nothing. "That bridge isn't going to fall down."

But she'd been complaining about that bridge for years.

"It means it's probably time for y'all to think about moving." Dad hadn't shouted, but he might as well have. His words ricocheted around the room like shrapnel.

"Move?" Now my hands were all bouncy and jittery too.

Mama reached over and put her hands on my knees to keep me from vibrating right out of my chair. But she didn't tell Dad that we would never leave Boutin.

What kind of Robichaux would I be if I left? We were born here and we died here, and in between was life on the water and family get-togethers.

"This town is going underwater, like Isle de Jean Charles. The newspaper today called us climate refugees," he said.

"You aren't anything," Nonnie snapped. "You don't live here."

"But the water will go down." We flooded. The water went down.

"Maybe. Maybe not. Louisiana loses, like, a football field of land an hour or something," Dad said. "It was only a matter of time. Eventually, everyone is going to have to leave."

Adrenaline spiked through me, fight or flight, and I knew exactly which one it was going to be.

Fight. For home, it would always be fight.

But the rational part of my brain knew that eventually, it would have to be flight, because when you picked a fight with Mother Nature, she always won.

The same was pretty much true if you picked a fight with Nonnie.

"You first," she said, tossing her cards on the table and leaving the room.

For a little while, this kitchen had been back to normal, full of food and laughter and hope. I hadn't wanted to be anywhere else. Now, I couldn't sit still. I tossed my cards on top of Nonnie's and followed her outside.

She was sitting on the top step of the porch looking out over the backyard. "Have I ever told you about Great-Uncle Clovis?"

I sat down next to her. "Is he the one who ate all the green persimmons right before Mass?"

"No, that was my Great-Uncle Clarence. Lord, it's a wonder they ever let any of us back in church after that."

That story was one of my favorites. I'd retold it in second grade (to much laughter, I might add) and Mrs. Debenedetto made me sit out at recess for using "foul language." I hadn't minded. Because after I told that story, everyone in class had forgotten about Maddie dropping her lunch tray. Mama had to explain that not all of Nonnie's stories were repeatable. Nonnie had called Mrs. Debenedetto an old Puritan, which I had most definitely not repeated.

"This is your papa's great uncle. Now, when Great-Uncle Clovis was a young man, he got lost in the swamps up the bayou a ways."

I tried to ignore the way my heart was pounding out a panic. Nonnie's stories had a way of making things better, and I desperately needed this one to.

"The whole town thought he was lost for good, but he stumbled out a couple weeks later, skinny and scarred up. Said he'd found the biggest cypress tree in the state of Louisiana. He couldn't get his arms even halfway around it."

I stared out over my backyard and let Nonnie's words fill the empty spaces that had opened up when my dad had used the word *move*. Boutin was my home.

"See, trees have their own language, and Clovis spoke it. He said the cypress had fallen in love with the stars—that's why it was so tall. He also said that tree told him how to get home. That the other trees showed him the way out." Nonnie looked me dead in the eye. "Great-Uncle Clovis was a tree whisperer."

I used to believe every story Nonnie ever told me. And right then I wanted to believe in a cypress tree that loved the stars. I wanted to believe that everything would be okay. But I was old enough to know better. "How much of that story is even true?"

"Honey, every single story has a little bit of truth and a whole lot of lie."

But I didn't want lies. And Nonnie could read that in my face.

"What does it matter? It's a dang good story either way. What I do know is that Great-Uncle Clovis was lost and then he wasn't. And not too long after that the timber company cut down a cypress with thirteen hundred rings. A piece of it is in the sawmill museum over in Patterson if you don't believe me."

That tree had existed way before the United States, and they'd killed it. "I don't want a story about destroying things. What was the point of it anyway?"

"All of a sudden my stories have to have a point? Look, Great-Uncle Clovis was a Robichaux. And Robichauxs always find their way home."

I knew exactly where home was. I wasn't the one leaving—it was. I had only just learned about the missing parts of Boutin, and now they were telling me we were too late to save it. If it was that serious, this was the only thing people should have been talking about.

"I don't want tall tales. I want the truth."

"About what?"

"Everything. Why didn't you tell me?"

"Baby girl, I thought you listened to my stories."

I'd spent my whole life collecting her words.

"I'm always telling you about places I played as a kid that are now underwater. I showed you the Old Cemetery. And Papa died three years ago and look at that cemetery now."

But I hadn't fully realized how real and close it was. I'd thought it was just part of her stories. I couldn't—didn't want to—imagine my home drifting away on the tide.

And people were just expecting us to leave it, and each other. That was a lot of tradition left behind to float away. That was a lot of history and stories scattered into the wind.

"I didn't really understand," I said. "And now Boutin—"

Most of the houses in Boutin were on the other side of bridges. If they didn't fix them, people would have to move to stay safe. Move where? How far would we have to go? The barrier islands that used to protect us were gone, so our weather worsened. When we were gone, the hurricanes would move farther inland. At what point would it stop? Would the ocean eventually knock at Baton Rouge's door? Alexandria's? How long could New Orleans last?

I couldn't believe that where I'd grown up was no longer worth fighting for, worth saving.

When people talked about abandoning a town, what they were really talking about was abandoning its people. And the fact that my state was rapidly sinking didn't even make the national news.

Last year Mrs. Vaughn showed us pictures of ghost towns. I'd felt lonely looking at all those abandoned buildings. But those were out West, mining towns that dried up when the gold did.

There would be nothing dried or left behind in Boutin. If no one did anything to stop it, it would simply sink. And Boutin would become just like Eternal Rest Cemetery: full of ghosts, then full of water.

"I'm just so angry."

"Glad to have you join us. I've been angry for fifty years."

But I didn't want to be angry.

I wanted my mama to always sing while she washed the dishes, little wisps of hair falling out of her ponytail and around her face. I wanted Nonnie to forever tell her stories, talk gruffly while slipping me something sweet. I wanted the mist to rise over the bayou in the fall. I wanted potlucks down at the church, and the old men sitting outside the Shrimp Shed telling tall tales, and dances after the Blessing of the Fleet. I wanted all the wonderful parts of home to still be here when I grew up.

And now, somebody was telling me they wouldn't.

Chapter Seven

Saturday morning Mrs. Millie answered the door before we'd finished knocking. She was sitting in a wheelchair. Her face was folded in on itself several times, and her gray hair was curled tight. "Jillie, love, I can't believe how big you've gotten!"

"Hey, Mrs. Millie." My words were a little muffled, as she'd pulled me down into a huge hug. The cast on her arm pressed into my back.

"And you must be Susie's daughter. You look just like her."

Maddie, who'd jumped at the chance to get away from her little brother for the day, beamed.

"I hope you're up for company," said Mama. She'd tagged along to help Nonnie with a few chores.

"Honey, I'd die of boredom if no one came to visit." Mrs. Millie led us into her living room. Colorful afghans were thrown over everything that stayed still, and a couple of things that didn't. A large tabby cat glared at us from the other side of the room.

"We're just going to run by Dell's and get you a few things," Mama said. "You got a list?"

"And is common sense on it?" Nonnie pushed through the front door. "You shouldn't have been up on that ladder and you know it."

"Don't you lecture me, Wanda Robichaux. You do plenty you shouldn't and everyone knows it. If they're selling common sense down at Dell's, better buy yourself double."

Both ladies cackled. Mama grinned and rolled her eyes. Maddie shrugged at me.

I hoped I had as good a time when I was old as those two seemed to have.

"The list's on the kitchen counter," said Mrs. Millie. "And bring the girls and me some of those lemon squares while you're at it." She winked at me. "My running days are on hold."

"Are these Janelle Guidry's lemon squares?"

"Yes indeed."

Mama snagged one from the platter. "For the road. I'll be back in a bit."

Mama and Nonnie headed out the front door, and Maddie and I hovered in the middle of the living room.

"What do you need us to do?" I asked.

"Nothing but keep me company. Lettie Domingue said you were asking about Cooper's Dock. Now that's a name I hadn't heard in a long time."

I told her about Ida Labatut's house flooding and the pictures scattered across my dresser.

"Would you like to look at some of my pictures?" she asked.

"If you don't mind." I'd started looking at Mrs. Labatut's pictures every night before I went to bed. I wanted to see more of Boutin the way it had been.

"There's nothing an old lady likes so well as looking at pictures of herself before her face deflated," she said. "They're in the cabinet over there."

I grabbed two photo albums and brought them over to the couch. Maddie and I sat next to Mrs. Millie, and I opened the first one.

Black-and-white photos filled the pages. I looked closer at one that showed two rows of kids sitting on a weather-beaten front porch. "Is this your family?"

"That's them." Mrs. Millie pointed a gnarled finger at a little girl wearing a plain dress, hair braided into two pigtails. "I'm right here. I was born in that house, smack-dab in the middle of eleven children, and though we never had much money, we never went hungry either. Plenty of fish and shrimp and game out here, and the thing I remember most about my childhood was being happy. I remember running wild beneath the oak and cypress trees, swimming in the bayou, getting into mud fights with my brothers and picking blackberries with my sisters. I remember my mama's fig preserves and the way my daddy always smelled like cedar and tobacco."

There was so much that the picture couldn't show. Mrs. Millie looked out the window, and I wondered if she was seeing the way the world was then or the way it was now.

"We didn't take a lot of pictures back then."

Every single moment of my childhood had been documented; Mrs. Millie had to rely mostly on memory.

And when that failed, her stories would be gone.

"Mrs. Millie, would you mind telling your story on camera?" I wasn't even sure what I was going to do with it, but it felt necessary to save it while I had the chance. I couldn't stop the water from rising or the bridges from being condemned. But this was something I could do.

"I don't mind a bit," she said. "Luckily Janelle did my hair yesterday."

I took out my phone and nodded once I'd hit RECORD.

"I graduated from Boutin High School," Mrs. Millie said with a wistful smile. "Did all my years of schooling there. I even rode out Hurricane Betsy in the school."

"Really?" Maddie asked. She turned to me. "Until Katrina, it had been one of the deadliest storms. It came right up the Mississippi River and Bayou Lafourche."

Maddie's mind was like a camera. If she saw a fact, her brain took a picture of it.

"Weird that the school survived that storm and not this flood," I said.

"They sheltered people at the high school," Mrs.

Millie continued. "It got eerie quiet when the eye passed, but when the winds kicked up again, every window in the classroom where we were hunkered down blew in. It was terrifying."

But this story made me feel better. If the school could come back from that, it could come back from this.

"We rode out Hurricane Andrew in there too."

"Nonnie said Hurricane Andrew was one of the worst storms she'd ever seen," I said.

Mrs. Millie nodded. "It was pretty bad. Had to rebuild most of our houses from the ground up. The stilts under our houses keep the water out, but when the wind gets up like it did during Andrew, they swayed like grass stalks. Many of them just toppled on over. We lost a few people, though not as many as it could have been." She crossed herself. "I've never seen a man possessed like your daddy was then."

It took me a second to realize she was talking to me. "My dad?"

"Yes, ma'am. Your daddy was a kid then, maybe sixteen or so? But he was a man on fire. The storm was still here when he was out on the roads with his chain saw cutting them clear. He banged on doors to make sure those inside were safe. He helped men reshingle their roofs and pushed trees off cars." She smiled at me. "That is one thing I've always been able to say about your daddy. He helped people. If he knew someone who needed something, and he could help, he did. Always.

No matter how tired he was or how hard the job. That's a good man right there."

My dad had missed last year's science fair and Christmas program. Mrs. Millie knew a different version of my dad than I did.

But I couldn't stop myself from thinking—could he be that version with us?

Maddie stopped on a picture of a family picnic. Several blankets, covered with both food and kids, were spread out on the grass in the shade of several large oaks. Across the road behind them ran a bayou, tinged green and dotted with cypress trees adorned with Spanish moss. "Where's this?"

"That's the grove of dead trees out past Bayou Road. That's what happens when salt water flows into fresh water. It kills the trees. We used to picnic out there all the time, back before the ground turned soggy and then went underwater completely."

I knew the place, but there was no way I would have recognized it. Now it was nothing but dead trunks rising out of the water, all color leached out. I thought about Nonnie's story and wondered if that made the stars sad. If Great-Uncle Clovis the tree whisperer had still been alive, would he have heard the trees asking for help?

"Will you leave?" I asked. I hadn't been able to put last night's conversation out of my mind. It was hard to deny that Boutin was going underwater when I was looking at the evidence right here.

She sighed. "I never thought I would. I was born here. But my daughter is worried, and my doctor is all the way up in Thibodaux. I can't drive myself while I'm wearing this cast, and I hate to ask my neighbors. I know they'd help, but I also know they're busy. So moving would be heartbreaking but convenient. I'm not getting younger. Not that I'm not healthy. I'm in good shape for my age." She glared at me, in case I was going to suggest otherwise. I was not.

The need to preserve these stories was a burning I felt in my chest. I wanted this to matter. I wanted people to see that we mattered, that we were worth saving.

~

I watched Lucy from the window as she chased a frog through the swampy parts of our yard. Nonnie was going to fuss if the dog brought all that mud in the house, but I let her splash. I liked frogs too. Their music was the lullaby I fell asleep to every night. And they adapted. They hopped on land and swam in water.

Maybe my dad was like that. Maybe he was one way with other people and one way with us. Mrs. Millie knew a man who dropped everything to help others. The dad I knew was too busy for his family.

Nonnie said there was a little truth in every story. I very much wanted to know the truth about my dad. Maybe then I'd know how I felt about him. Because most days how I felt was such a tangle of different-colored threads that I knew I'd never make any sense out of the mess.

Dad had tucked the few things he'd saved from the flood into our storage shed. I stopped my pacing long enough to listen. I could hear Maddie in the kitchen talking to Nonnie, so when I was sure everyone was too busy to notice me, I went into the shed.

I didn't much like the storage shed, probably because so many critters liked it a lot. Mice lived in there, and a whole lot of spiders, and sometimes snakes. I wasn't afraid of critters—though I wasn't in a hurry to get snake bit or anything. But I didn't enjoy them surprising me, and it was dark and dirty in the shed, and I didn't want to accidentally grab a fistful of spiders.

Dad's boxes were the newest additions to our junk, so they were mostly clean and close to the door.

It made me sad to see the too-few boxes containing his entire life. Three boxes for the kitchen, one that simply read MISCELLANEOUS. And one that had my name on it.

I listened again to make sure I was alone before opening the lid.

My face stared up at me from several cheap frames—me in kindergarten, me at ten holding a redfish. There were stacks of pictures I'd drawn or colored, a stuffed tiger I'd left five years ago. At the very bottom I found a small framed picture of us as a family. I was probably two, and my parents were impossibly young, all of us grinning like fools at what looked like a Mardi Gras parade.

My dad and I had the exact same smile.

I put the picture back in the box. None of this stuff had been damaged by water.

"I packed that box first."

I jumped at Dad's voice. I'd been too busy trying to puzzle this together to hear him walk in. I wiggled the stuffed tiger. "I'd forgotten about this."

"He was sitting in your room."

My room. He'd had a room for me in his new house that I'd never seen. Why?

He kept a box of memories but was always too busy to make new ones. Why was it easier to love us from a distance? Was the idea of us better than the reality?

I wasn't brave like my mama or tough like Nonnie. I didn't ask my dad any of those questions. I was too afraid of the answers.

Instead, I carefully packed the box back up and went inside to see if Lucy wanted a walk.

Chapter Eight

I wish my mom would let me have a dog," Maddie muttered. She buried her face in Lucy's neck. Lucy wagged her tail and looked just as smitten as Maddie.

The three of us were sitting on the back porch. The sky was purple south of us, but it wasn't raining yet.

"You have a little brother. It's sort of the same thing."

"Reed is barely housebroken. And he's not even a little bit cuddly, so it's not the same thing at all."

A spoonbill floated over our backyard, its wings pink against the coming storm.

Mother Nature was my favorite artist. She used all the best colors.

Ms. Wilson said the Caminada Project helped birds. Had it helped this spoonbill? Was it here only because people had saved that beach?

I thought about how, like ripples across water, one thing changed many things. Louisiana flooded. So my dad came here. And Lucy.

I scratched Lucy's neck. She was starting to fit right in.

"So what is Aunt Nonnie saying about it?" Maddie asked.

We were, of course, talking about the bridges. It was all Boutin was talking about. At school the Carolton kids were talking about Thanksgiving break and video games and some kid called Toots who could burp the LSU fight song.

Most of what Nonnie said was absolutely not repeatable. I translated. "That those state boys couldn't find their butts with both hands. And that they would have to drag her out of Boutin."

Mama'd had to intervene then because I went to pacing and stewing. "It's not a mandatory evacuation." She'd put her arms around me and rubbed my back and I'd felt a little better.

We'd had a very bad flood, but we were getting back on our feet. The school would reopen and everything would go right back to normal.

Only I was learning that Boutin's normal wasn't so normal after all.

"My dad said this was just like last year when they said that hurricane was going to drop twenty-five inches of rain on us and then we only got, like, five," Maddie said.

I hoped Maddie's dad was right. I wasn't ready to give up.

"So you never did explain why you videoed Mrs. Millie's story," Maddie said.

"I'm collecting them." I'd spent my life listening to stories—now I wanted to gather and guard them.

"Why?"

"I have to save them."

"Save them for what?"

Maddie asked questions—that's what she did. She asked questions and found answers. But today it made me mad. I shouldn't have had to explain to her how important it was. Boutin was her home too.

But she'd never loved it like I did. I couldn't imagine myself living anywhere else, but Maddie spent most of her time imagining herself in faraway places.

"I don't know!" I snapped.

Maddie blinked. "Sorry. I was just curious."

"Well, I haven't figured it out yet." Because this seemed a whole lot bigger—a whole lot more important—than I was. "But I don't have to do anything with them—they just have to exist."

Stories were the way we saved what was temporary—they made the mortal immortal.

Lucy brought Maddie a ball, and she threw it. Lucy was lucky she didn't have much else to worry about. "Have you heard anything about school?"

"What about it?" Maddie took the ball, now covered in slobber and grass, from Lucy and tossed it again.

"Like when it might reopen?"

In the brief flash of surprise on Maddie's face, I realized she'd thought I meant Carolton. I was angry again. "You know, our school."

"It's only been a couple of weeks," Maddie said. "It's going to take a lot longer than that. Why are you in such a hurry?"

I glared at her. "Why aren't you?"

"I mean, it's not like they split us up. We're with our friends. Mary Catherine's cousin lives in Denham Springs and she had to move to a school where she doesn't know anyone at all."

"But don't you want to get back?"

"Of course. It's just—Carolton has a lot of stuff we don't have, like robotics club. And book club. And the high school has advanced classes." Lucy dropped the ball in Maddie's lap, and she threw it again.

Of course Maddie already knew all that. She'd started her college fund in fourth grade. And I should have been happy for her. She was getting things she'd always wanted. But I was losing everything, and her excitement felt like betrayal.

"It isn't our school." I didn't know how else to explain it, and I shouldn't have had to. It wasn't home.

"I miss Boutin Middle too, but it's also okay if I'm excited about new things."

I sighed. "I know it is." But even if my head knew that, my heart didn't. Because my heart belonged to Boutin. And I thought hers should too.

Maddie's mama came to pick her up just about the time it started raining. Lucy and I stood on the front porch and watched the raindrops ripple the surface of the puddles lining the driveway. It thundered somewhere close. Lucy barked at it.

I felt a lot like the storm—gray and rainy, desperate to thunder loudly at everything.

Lucy barked again, this time at Dad's truck pulling in. She waited until he'd opened his door before dashing out to greet him. I shouldn't have felt abandoned. She was his dog. She pranced around his feet as he hauled several large grocery bags out of the back of his truck.

"I had to go to Carolton," Dad told me as he climbed the porch steps. "Dell's Grocery isn't what it used to be."

"We make do," I told him. I didn't tell him that Mama stopped in Carolton on her way home from work at least twice a month to get all the things Dell's no longer carried. He didn't get to say ugly things about Boutin. If he didn't like it here, he could go home.

Except that he couldn't. I was a terrible, awful person.

I was going to be better. "What is all that stuff?"

"I'm making my famous turtle sauce piquant," he said. "I was hoping you'd help. Thought you might like to learn how to make it."

I thought about Mrs. Millie's story, and I wondered

what else I didn't know about my dad. He was here now, asking to spend time with me.

So I said yes.

He blinked. Smiled. "Great." He climbed the rest of the stairs, bags swinging. His smile was a bit befuddled. "Great," he said again.

I waited on the porch while Lucy got herself thoroughly wet. I made her shake off real good before letting her in the house because neither of us wanted Nonnie mad. She was probably already in a tizzy over Dad using her kitchen.

Mama was folding towels on the couch. Nonnie held an unread newspaper and stared distrustfully at the rather loud banging coming from the kitchen.

"He says you two are cooking us dinner."

"Yep." I grabbed a towel and attempted to dry Lucy. "He wants to teach me how to make turtle sauce piquant."

Mama looked up. "Wow. That's his secret recipe. He never would tell me what was in it."

A teeny tiny thread of light spread from the center of my chest to the tips of my fingers.

Nonnie opened her newspaper. Mama folded another towel. Lucy curled up on the other end of the couch, opposite Mama, and Nonnie didn't even fuss.

Dad was at the kitchen sink when I walked in, vegetables and cans strewn all over the counter. "I don't know where anything is."

"What do you need?"

"A large pot to boil the turtle, and the big cast-iron skillet. Plus cutting boards and knives."

I opened the door to the small pantry. "Big pots are here." Nonnie kept her gumbo pot on the floor because it was too tall for most cabinets. Cooking big was a Louisiana tradition. If you weren't cooking for at least ten, you weren't really cooking.

"The best way to cook a sauce piquant is outside over a burner," he told me. "But today is not the day for that." He filled the gumbo pot with water. "First we boil the turtle—just a little while to get it tender. It's better to get all the vegetables cut up before you make the roux."

"Nonnie says the same thing."

"I'm glad we agree on something."

I snagged an onion from the pile and started chopping.

"Do you need help with that?" Dad asked. He eyed my misshapen pieces of onion. "I cut them like this—"

He reached toward the onion, but I slid it out of reach. "Both Mama and Nonnie have shown me how. And they said you really just have to practice and figure out what way works best for you."

He went back to his bell pepper. "That's good advice."

We chopped in silence after that. He dumped the flour and oil together to start the roux. "You're in charge of this now." He handed me the spoon. I started stirring.

"I'm sorry," he said after a while.

I looked up from the roux. Dad was prodding the turtle and not looking at me. "For?"

"A lot of things? I'm not perfect, but I am trying."

"Mama already told me that."

"Your mama is a good woman."

"I'm not the one who needs telling." I went back to stirring. The roux was slowly turning from blond to café au lait.

Dad peered over the lip of the pot. "Looks good. Still got a ways to go though. I like my roux really dark."

"Me too." For some reason, dark roux tasted the way I imagined fall would, if fall had a taste—smoky and rich.

"You know, it wasn't all bad. We had a lot of fun too. Do you remember the time we took you fishing at Stelley's pond? You got so excited every time you caught a fish. I'm pretty sure you just caught the same little thing over and over again. We had to drag you away once it got too dark to see, but we couldn't pry the pole out of your hand. So we let you hold on to it, and I carried you to the truck on my shoulders, and you drew back to cast the line into the darkness and buried the hook in my butt."

He grinned. The steam from the kitchen was starting to fog up the windows as the rain pinged off the glass.

"I yowled and nearly dropped you, and you started crying, and your mama was laughing so hard she could barely stand up." When I didn't say anything, he asked, "You really don't remember that?"

"I only remember living with Nonnie and Papa." I only remembered him being gone.

He looked sad then, and I felt a little guilty for telling him the truth. So I did what Nonnie would do.

I gave him a story.

"One time Papa was fixing the dryer, and the screwdriver slipped and sliced his hand open. It was bad. Blood everywhere."

I widened my eyes like Nonnie did at the gross parts.

"He grabbed a rag from the laundry basket and wrapped it quick tight. Mama came close to fainting dead away—that's how much blood there was. Nonnie made Papa go to the hospital even though he didn't want to."

I remembered most of this story from when it happened. The other parts I remembered from the retellings.

"When the doctor at the Carolton hospital removed the rag from Papa's hand, it was Nonnie's turn to almost faint dead away. Because what Papa thought was a rag was a pair of Nonnie's underwear!"

I put a lot of enthusiasm into that last sentence, just the way Nonnie did to show it was the best part of the story.

Dad laughed. And laughed. His shoulders bounced and his stomach wiggled and he looked like an accordion, squeezing out happiness.

Making people laugh is one of the best feelings in the whole world.

"Man, I wish I'd been there to see that," he finally said.

We'd had a lot of good times. He'd missed all of them. "Me too."

He wiped his eyes. "I needed that."

I felt a little bit of my anger slip away. "Nonnie is full of stories like that." And they could patch up just about anything.

"She's full of a lot of things," Dad muttered.

Yep. Like grit and grump and love that leaked right around her sharp edges.

"I guess it's time I revealed the recipe's secret ingredient." He reached into the cabinet and pulled down the canister of coffee. "I don't guess I can ask you to keep it a secret from Nonnie."

"Are you kidding?" I said. "I can't wait to be able to cook something better than she does."

Dad's laughter filled the kitchen again, and for the first time since he'd arrived, I didn't feel so claustrophobic.

"Maybe I could pick you up from school one day this week?" he asked later as the turtle sauce piquant was bubbling merrily away on the stove.

This time, I said yes.

Chapter Nine

On Tuesday we had a guest speaker in science. Ms. Wilson had warned us several times to be on our best behavior and not embarrass her, so I'd started thinking this man ate middle schoolers for breakfast or something. Only he was a she, and she wasn't wearing a white coat like all the scientists did on TV.

She was wearing jeans and a T-shirt with *Wetlands Discovery Center* written across the front. She was Black, and her braided hair was pulled back in a ponytail. She wasn't that much taller than Nonnie.

"Good morning!" she said after Ms. Wilson had taken roll and sat at her desk. "I'm Dr. Evelyn Nelson, an ecologist with Lumcon." At the puzzled looks on some faces, she smiled. "Lumcon stands for the Louisiana Universities Marine Consortium, and our team is just one of many studying Louisiana's environmental problems."

I tried not to frown and put on what my mama called my grump face, but I was getting sick and tired of people talking about our problems like they were just that—problems with no solutions. The water was rising permanently, not just with floods, and the state had decided we weren't worth saving, and I was not in the least little bit interested in hearing how bad things were—because after spending most of my life not understanding, I was getting a very clear picture of just how bad things were.

I wanted someone instead to talk about how good things could be.

"Ecology deals with balance. We're all connected, from the way we fish this land, to the mosquito, to the grass it lays its eggs in. If one thing gets out of balance, it ripples out, causing other problems for other organisms. No place is that more visible than Louisiana. Our coast is eroding. The causes are both human and natural, but one cannot argue that the consequences aren't devastating. As the coast pulls back, we lose not only land but plants, insects, birds, and animals. We lose a way of life."

Except most of the people in this room weren't losing their way of life—just those of us from Boutin.

"It's not just the job of scientists to protect this land," Dr. Nelson continued. "We all have a responsibility."

Was she only saying we *should* do something about it, or did she really believe we could? How did you stop water from stealing your home?

"I grew up in Louisiana, but I spent several years in

Brazil. They're also dealing with coastal erosion. I'm telling you all this because I want you to know that you, we, are not alone. Not alone in this experience, and not alone in this fight."

Boutin was not alone. Dad had made it seem like there was nothing more we could do, that we had to accept what was happening and just walk away. Dr. Nelson was saying we could fight. That we had the power to change things.

She wasn't telling me not to worry. She wasn't telling me it would all work out. She was telling me that this was actually happening and that I had a right to be upset—and a part to play in the solution. I looked around. Derek was half asleep. Maddie was taking notes. But this wasn't something to memorize for a test. This was real life. My life.

My bones went to vibrating, but this time, it wasn't because I was worried. It was because I was ready. Hopeful. Excited.

Dr. Nelson pointed to her T-shirt. "I am part of the new Wetlands Discovery Center project. Scientists, business owners, teachers like Ms. Wilson here, and community members are working together to create a learning center that will serve to educate about our wetlands." Ms. Wilson stood up to pass out colorful brochures. I took one and stared at the pictures of fishing boats and roseate spoonbills and marsh grass. Snapshots of home. The address was in Houma, almost a couple hours' drive away. "Exhibits on wildlife, communities, and culture will fill the building, and I invite you to visit when it opens in the spring."

She glanced around the room, and when she looked at me, I felt like she was talking only to me.

"I also help organize volunteers to help pick up trash and plant marsh grass, and we would love to have you. These may not seem like life-altering acts, but I promise you, small acts accumulate into larger ones, and if every person in this state took a small responsibility for the health and welfare of it, for its future, we would be in much better shape than we are now. I believe we can be better. I believe Louisiana is a place worth preserving, and I believe it has a hopeful future. And I believe it starts with us. Thank you."

Chill bumps blossomed down my arms, and my chest tightened. Dr. Nelson said there was hope. She said people were fighting this.

Maddie leaned across the aisle. "Are you okay?" she whispered.

Did the storm show on my face? "I'm okay."

You know how sometimes it rains really hard even when the sun is out? My insides felt a little like that. Part of me was swampy and scared and angry about what was happening. Part of me was hopeful and excited because Dr. Nelson said people were trying to stop it. She'd said we could help. I could help.

I didn't have to wait until I was older, which was

good, because we were running out of time. Too many people waited for someone else to do the work. I wasn't going to be like that.

Ever since the flood I'd felt pretty helpless, just like a turtle that has flipped over on its back. Its legs just claw at the air but it doesn't go anywhere at all. And it was like Dr. Nelson was the one to flip me back over, because she said I could do something.

I wanted to help Louisiana, and I thought my chest might burst with the wanting.

"Well, she was awesome," Mina said as we left class. She fell in beside me. "A Black female scientist. In Carolton." Mina looked about how I felt, all hope and excitement. Today she was wearing leopard-print tennis shoes, and she practically floated six inches above the linoleum.

"I know. And she's been to Brazil. And she's fighting coastal erosion." I was aware that I was mostly babbling, but Mina didn't seem to care. I peeled away and headed to my next class.

"See you at lunch!" Mina shouted.

I let my idea simmer until lunchtime, but by the time the bell rang to end fourth period, I knew what I was going to do. And I had to tell someone.

"You asked what I was going to do with the stories,"

I said as I met up with Maddie on the way to the cafeteria.

"And you said it was enough that they simply exist," she answered.

"I've changed my mind. I think—" I stopped, wondering if I should even say it aloud. Who was I to think I could change anything? I was a thirteen-year-old girl from a town so small it wasn't on most maps. A town that might not exist at all in twenty years. My idea needed someone older and wiser and smarter and louder. Someone people would listen to. Maybe saying the words would shatter the magic. I spit them out before I lost my courage, while Dr. Nelson's words still made me feel strong. "I'm going to email Dr. Nelson and see if she would use the pictures and stories at the Wetlands Discovery Center. That way people will know what is happening here. That way I'm saving them for a bigger purpose."

"Oral histories?" Mina asked. Her face peeped up over my shoulder. I hadn't seen her standing in line behind us. She had a way of sneaking up on a person. She was like a quiet little cat.

"Yeah," I said. "Oral histories." I explained more about the pictures I'd found, the stories I was collecting.

"Can I help?"

"Why would you want to?" I asked. Maddie elbowed me, but Mina didn't seem bothered by the question.

"I like stories. And old pictures."

I wanted to say no. She wasn't from Boutin, so she really couldn't understand. And I kind of wanted to do this all by myself. But I'd seen her after hearing Dr. Nelson speak. I could use Mina's kind of enthusiasm.

"I have a good camera," she added. "We can go around Boutin and take pictures of the way those places look now."

I smiled. "That's actually a really great idea." Side by side, people could see the devastation firsthand. And we would save stories. I'd always believed in their magic, and we needed all of that we could get.

~

I barely made it through the rest of the day. I wanted to get home, to get started, to tell Mama and Nonnie all about my ideas. I was even excited about telling my dad. Now we'd have something to talk about on the forty-minute ride home.

I found Maddie just outside school in the bus line. Two buses were all it took to shuttle our students from home to here. The elementary school kids were already on the bus. They'd pick up the high school kids on the way out.

"My dad's coming to pick me up," I told Maddie as she waited to get on the bus. I hadn't said those words in a really long time. It actually felt pretty good.

She looked around the parking lot for his truck. I'd

already seen that he wasn't here yet. He needed to hurry if I was going to get anything done before dark.

"That's good." Maddie climbed the bus steps. "See you tomorrow, then!"

I waved and watched the Boutin buses pull out. Watched the Carolton buses pull out. Watched the parking lot empty.

No Dad. I texted him. No answer.

I sat down on the curb. Waited fifteen more minutes. Called. Got his voice mail.

"Jillian!" Mina was carrying a bag almost as big as she was.

"Hey."

"Do you need a ride?" she asked.

Was she offering to drive me all the way to Boutin? I hadn't wanted to make friends when I'd first come to Carolton, but it looked like Mina was going to make that impossible. I couldn't help but like her. "No thanks. My dad is on his way."

I hoped my dad was on his way. He showed up for Lucy, he showed up during Hurricane Andrew. Surely he could show up for me.

"You sure?"

"Yes. I'm fine." Her dad probably never forgot to pick her up. Shame sat right down beside me and practically screamed my humiliation at Mina.

Could he really have forgotten?

"Okay. See you tomorrow." Mina jogged over to a

waiting car, tossed her bag in the back, and climbed in after it.

The principal came out of the school a little while later. "Did you miss the bus home?"

"My dad's running late."

His warm, kind smile made me even more ashamed to be lying to him. Because at this point I knew my dad wasn't going to show. "It happens to the best of us. You're from Boutin, right?"

"Yes, sir."

"I'm Mr. Saucier."

"Jillian Robichaux."

"Nice to meet you, Jillian."

No flicker of recognition. No asking about Nonnie or Mama. I'd never gone to school where the adults didn't know me and my people. All that hope and excitement I'd been feeling leaked right out, as if someone had pulled a plug.

"Glad you're here."

"Thank you," I said, because my mama taught me to be polite. But in that moment, I wanted to be anywhere but stranded in Carolton.

Thankfully, Mr. Saucier went back inside. I checked my phone one more time—no text or call from Dad. I would have to call Mama.

And then Nonnie was there. "I had some errands to run in Carolton and thought I'd drive by, check out the school. And lo and behold, I find you here."

I figured this was another one of Nonnie's tall tales, but I wasn't going to call her on it. "Dad forgot me." And there were the tears, ready to ambush me. I willed myself not to cry. Robichauxs were tough.

"Good thing I took this detour, then. Hop in. Have I ever told you the story about Uncle Pete and the one-eyed catfish?"

She didn't say a word about Dad, didn't do anything but what she had done for my entire life: She showed up.

Lucy met me at the front door. It didn't matter if I'd been gone all day or for only five minutes—she was glad to see me. Her tail went to wagging, and she shuffled her feet back and forth, antsy for pets. I dropped my book sack and folded to the floor.

"Hey, girl," I said, scratching her ears. She sat down in front of me. I leaned forward and buried my face in her neck, rubbing my hands up and down her sides. Maybe Lucy knew I was upset. Maybe she just needed the balance. Whatever the reason, she reached up and rested her paw on my shoulder.

"Thanks," I said, still running my hands along her ribs. "I think I needed that."

I stood up and grabbed my stuff. Lucy followed me into my room. I tossed my book sack in the corner. I hadn't been able to talk about Dr. Nelson and my story project when Nonnie had picked me up from school. I'd been too full of storm clouds, and I hadn't wanted any of them to rain on what had been my excitement. Nonnie had told me stories the whole way home, and I'd been able to curl up inside her words and forget for just a bit how I'd felt sitting stranded on the curb of a still-new school in a strange town. But now that I was alone (well, not actually alone, Lucy reminded me as she flopped down on the floor), I couldn't stop the mad from thundering in.

I was mostly mad at myself. Today had been a good day—no, a great day—and it would have stayed that way if I hadn't agreed to let Dad come and pick me up from school. I'd said no the first time he'd asked because assuming he didn't care enough to show was better than knowing it for sure. But then the story about my dad had made me think there was a chance. I should have remembered what Nonnie said about most stories—a little truth, a lot of lie.

I stopped pacing and stood in front of Mrs. Labatut's pictures, which were still strewn across the top of my dresser. Those were the stories I wanted to know about.

Lucy and I were still in my room when Dad got home. Mama was waiting for him in the living room.

"You forgot your daughter." Mama was trying to be quiet, but the walls were thin and I could hear her just fine. Nonnie had retreated to the kitchen, but I was pretty sure she was listening too. I knew Nonnie, and it was taking every single bit of willpower she had to stay in that kitchen instead of reaming out Dad.

It was nice having Mama and Nonnie in my corner.

"I didn't forget. I got tied up."

Lucy went to the door when she heard Dad's voice, but I didn't open it.

"Then you should have called me. She sat outside that school for almost an hour waiting on you."

"I'm sorry."

"She's spent most of her life waiting on you. You never show up."

"Nora, I'm doing my best. And I'm sorry."

Mama's phone rang. "Right now, your best is the worst. And it's not me you should be apologizing to."

Mama went onto the front porch to get better reception and answered her phone. A knock came at my door moments later.

Lucy whined.

I considered ignoring the knock, or pretending I forgot to answer. I did neither, but I did stand at the door instead of letting Dad inside.

"I'm really sorry about today," Dad said. Lucy stuck her head through the doorway, and Dad patted her. She squeezed past him and went into the living room. Maybe she was mad at him too. I liked thinking she was on my side. "The meeting with my boss lasted a lot longer than it was supposed to."

"It's okay." But it wasn't. I just didn't know how to put into words exactly what I was feeling.

"It won't happen again. I can pick you up tomorrow."

I wasn't going to fall for that again. "I'd rather ride the bus with Maddie."

Dad's face sort of deflated, and I tried to ignore my guilt. I hadn't done anything wrong. "I understand. When I was your age I would have rather been with my friends too."

He still didn't really get it. Sometimes it felt like people heard me but they weren't actually listening.

"Okay, I'll let you get back to it."

I shut the door before he'd turned to walk away.

"I'm going for a drive," I heard Dad tell Nonnie. "Don't wait dinner on me."

"I wasn't planning on it."

I waited several more minutes to give Dad time to well and truly leave before coming out of my room. Mama was still outside on the phone.

"You're a spoiled little brat, aren't you?" I heard Nonnie say. I stopped where I was. I'd thought I'd heard my dad's truck pull out of the driveway. But there was an indulgent edge to her normal bluster, so I knew she couldn't be talking to him.

I stepped into the kitchen just as Nonnie slipped Lucy a piece of sausage. The dog was staring up at her with something like adoration.

"Aha!"

Nonnie jumped, then scowled at me. "What's gotten into you, sneaking in here and trying to scare me half to death?"

"You aren't afraid of the devil himself," I said. "And yet I think you're turning into an old softy."

"Oh, really? Just for that, no dinner for you."

"Fine. I didn't want any of your old cooking anyway. Just give it to Lucy."

"Give it to Lucy," Nonnie muttered under her breath. She finished chopping the sausage. "I made peanut butter cookies, if you think you can choke one down all right. Just don't spoil your dinner."

I grabbed a couple and folded myself into a chair at the kitchen table. Lucy moved from Nonnie's side to mine.

"You little opportunist," Nonnie told Lucy.

I didn't want to talk about Dad.

"We had a guest speaker in science today," I told Nonnie. And then I was off.

She let me wear myself out—she was good like that. When I seemed to finally run through my words, she put a bowl of potatoes in front of me and tossed in a stick of butter. Handed me an old-fashioned masher. "Put some of that energy to good use."

I took the masher. "You know you could probably do this faster with a mixer."

"Builds character."

"Can you get ahold of Ida Labatut? I think I need to ask permission to use those pictures."

"She won't care," Nonnie said. "But yes, I have her son's number."

"Will you talk on camera?" I asked. I wanted to save Nonnie's stories more than all the others. They were tucked safely inside me, but the world deserved those stories. We could all use a big dose of comfort, and Nonnie's stories were chock-full of that.

"I'm not good at that kind of stuff."

"You're kidding me, right? You tell stories better than anyone I know."

"Why don't you talk to Bud Talbot?" she suggested. "He likes talking about himself better than almost anything, and he's even older than I am."

"You're not that old," I told Nonnie.

"Tell that to my joints."

Lucy jumped up and raced into the living room seconds before Mama walked in the door.

My heart started pacing my rib cage the minute I saw Mama's face. "What's wrong?"

Nonnie turned from the stove, her forehead creased with concern. "Everything okay?"

But Mama was looking at me. "Janelle Guidry called me from the school board meeting."

"I didn't even know there was a meeting." We should have gone.

"There's always a meeting on the second Tuesday of the month," Mama told me.

"But if they were discussing the school reopening,

they should have told us so we could be there." Because surely they hadn't been talking about anything other than getting us back where we belonged.

Mama glanced at Nonnie once before sitting down next to me. "They aren't reopening the school. Ever. They're shutting Boutin schools down permanently."

Chapter Ten

On my way to school the next morning I saw a FOR SALE sign in the Pitres' front yard. That was like putting a vacancy sign on the *Titanic*.

The only new thing about the Pitres' house was the roof, which had been damaged in the last hurricane, and a few of the stilts, which had been replaced and now were a different color than the rest of them. The house did what houses should—kept them dry and warm—so it shouldn't really matter that the paint on the shutters was peeling off in strips or that the siding was faded. But it did.

Nobody was going to buy a weathered house in a sinking town without a school. But I wasn't giving up.

"They can't shut down the school," I said at lunch. The Boutin kids were settled into their chosen corner, and I set my tray on the table next to Maddie.

"I think they already have," Derek said.

"I mean, the pipes leaked in the bathroom and the ceiling had soft spots," Adam said.

"Maybe it wasn't a fancy school, but it was our school." I pulled a piece of paper out of my bag and handed it to him. "Sign the petition."

Derek laughed. "You think that will work?"

"I think it's better than doing nothing."

Maddie slid the paper over her way. "I'll sign it."

I knew how much Maddie would be giving up when we went back to Boutin—no robotics club, no honors classes. But she was fighting right beside me anyway. "Thanks."

Mina, who was sitting at the table behind us, leaned across the aisle and stuck her head next to mine. "You won't get very many signatures that way."

And I had just started liking that girl. "I didn't ask you." I did a passable impersonation of Nonnie's gruff.

Mina didn't seem bothered. "You'll have to go person to person. Lots of time for very little impact."

Mina wanted to help with my story project because she liked old pictures. To me it felt like throwing a life preserver around my disappearing community. She hadn't transferred schools. Her hometown hadn't been deemed too insignificant to save. I didn't care how much time getting signatures took. "Then I'll go person to person."

"Or," Mina said, "you could create a petition online and share the link and get thousands of signatures all at once."

I wanted to be annoyed at this Carolton kid butting

into my business yet again, but this was the second good idea she'd given me. "I can show you."

"Thanks." It looked like I was making friends in Carolton after all. That didn't mean I was settling in. We were going to get our school back.

"The petition is just the first step," I said. "There's a board meeting next month. We should all show up and speak."

"You can't just show up at a board meeting," Derek said.

"They're open to the public," Maddie explained. "Anyone can go."

"But not anyone can talk," Derek argued. "And they aren't going to listen to you."

Maybe not. But that wasn't going to stop me from trying.

I leaned across the aisle. "Eat fast and let's get started."

Mina grinned and shoved half a roll in her mouth. Maddie drank the last of her milk, and I took a couple more bites of mashed potatoes. Sometimes arming for battle meant cutting lunch short and heading to the library.

"Enjoy wasting your time," Derek said as we left.

"Enjoy watching us get this done." I marched out of the cafeteria attempting to look way more certain than I felt.

A group of eighth graders was sprawled out on the

sofa and chairs in the library's reading nook, but the computers were empty.

"Hey, Mrs. Landers," Mina said. "Can we use a computer?"

"Of course, dear." Mrs. Landers waved us in and continued shelving books.

"How do you know how to do this?" I asked Mina.

She slid in front of a computer and immediately pulled her legs up to sit crisscross applesauce. "Because last year I started a petition to increase the quality of school lunches."

Mina saw problems and wanted to be a part of the solution. I respected that.

"And how did that work out?" Maddie asked.

"You tell me," Mina said grimly. She clacked away at the keyboard and was quickly on a petition website. "Okay, here we go." She clicked a few boxes. "Name of the petition?"

"Reopen Boutin Schools," I said.

Mina typed. "People responsible for action?"

"The school district," Maddie answered.

"Great. Now we need a statement, like a paragraph or two on why this matters." She and Maddie both looked at me.

"That's going to take longer than the five minutes we have left of lunch. And I—" Why was it so hard to admit I couldn't do this all by myself? This had been my idea. I shouldn't plan big ideas that I couldn't do alone. But this wasn't just my school, and this mattered too much. "I'm going to need help."

A few more clicks and Mina stood up. "I saved it. You can finish it this weekend."

"We can," I corrected her. Because somewhere between the cafeteria and here, this had become part of my—our—project. *Operation Save Boutin*—its stories, its school, its way of life. And Derek might have been right—three middle school girls probably didn't have enough power to get all of that done. But we'd never know until we tried. "Maddie's spending the night tonight," I told Mina. "You should come too."

Mina beamed. "Great! But shouldn't you ask your parents first?"

"My mama won't care. And my dad . . ." Well, I could explain some of that on the bus ride home.

"It smells amazing in here!" I shouted as I dropped my book sack by the front door. Lucy hopped off the sofa and did a little victory dance around the living room. More people meant more potential for snacks. She sniffed us all thoroughly, spending an extra-long time inspecting Mina's Hawaiian-print tennis shoes.

"I have a cat," Mina explained. Lucy apparently forgave her that character flaw and allowed Mina to scratch her ears.

We trooped into the kitchen.

"Hi, Aunt Nonnie!"

Nonnie pulled away from the stove long enough to give Maddie a good long squeeze. "I don't think we've met," she told Mina.

"Mina is from Carolton," I said. "She's helping me with the project." That didn't sound exactly right. "And she's my friend." We'd spent the forty minutes on the bus talking about books (Maddie and Mina were both huge fantasy fans) and places we'd been. (Mina had been to so many states. I'd been to, like, four.) It had been nice to pretend things were normal for a while. Maddie and Mina had complained about their younger siblings, and I'd scrolled through my phone showing them pictures of Lucy.

"Nice to meet you, Mina. Now that reminds me," Nonnie said. She handed me a piece of paper. "Ida's number."

"Thanks! They're her pictures," I explained to Mina. "And I need to ask her if I can give them away before I offer them to Dr. Nelson." I stared at the number. "I'm going to call her now." Before I chickened out about the whole thing. I dialed the number and went to stand by the kitchen sink so I could look out the window. My stomach lurched and wobbled as it rang.

"Hello?"

My mouth went dry and I coughed a little. "Is Mrs. Labatut there?"

"Which one?" the voice asked.

"The old one." Oops. Nonnie made a choking noise behind me.

The voice laughed. "Well, I guess that's me. This is Ida."

"Sorry, Mrs. Labatut, I didn't mean it like that. It's Jillian Robichaux."

"Well hi, Jillian! It's all right. I am old. It's better than the alternative."

"How are you doing?" I asked.

"I miss my house," she said. "And I don't like Texas."

I didn't really know what to say to that. "I tried to find you at the church a couple days after the flood. I accidentally kept a few of your pictures."

"Pshaw. Keep them. I don't know what to do with the ones I have."

"Well, I have an idea." I explained about the Wetlands Discovery Center, the stories I was collecting. "I don't know if they'll want any of it." I tried to keep the worry out of my voice. I'd gotten my hopes up, and I didn't know what I would do if they said no. "But I wanted your permission before I offered them to the center."

"Of course, dear. Those pictures were never mine to begin with—they were Boutin's. And I'm thrilled someone might want them." She got quiet for a minute, and I could hear a TV in the background. "You're pretty impressive, Jillian Robichaux."

I blushed. "Thank you. For saying that and for the pictures."

But I didn't think I was impressive at all—just

determined. And desperate. And angry. Hopefully those would make up for all the things I wasn't.

We hung up. I wiped my palms on my pants. I joined Maddie and Mina at the kitchen table and grabbed a couple of cookies. Lucy parked herself under the table and waited for nibbles.

"All good?" Maddie asked.

"Yep. We can use them." I felt myself getting excited again. "We're getting the school reopened," I told Nonnie. Mama said a little swagger went a long way. I was practicing adding a tad of confidence to my words so that when I said them in front of the school board, they'd be more likely to listen.

"That explains the destructive look in your eye. You always got that look when you were little, right before you broke something valuable."

"We've started a petition," I told her, "and we're going to present it at the next board meeting. You'll sign it once it's live, right?"

"I'll be the first one." Nonnie looked over to Maddie, than back at me, her face thoughtful. "Well, I've never seen either one of you fail to do something once you put your minds to it. Two more stubborn girls I have never met."

"It's inherited," I told Mina. I only hoped I'd inherited the good things from them too.

She was happily munching her way through a cookie. "My dad says stubborn is what gets most things done."

“I’d have to agree with your dad on that one,” Nonnie said. “Speaking of dads. Maddie, did I ever tell you about the time your dad managed to get himself locked out of the house in nothing but a pair of rubber boots?”

Maddie coughed and spit crumbs all over the table and floor. Lucy happily cleaned up the mess. Maddie grinned once she got control of herself. “No. But oh my goodness, please tell me you’re going to share that story.”

Nonnie had a mischievous glint in her eye. “I think you’re old enough to hear this one.” And she launched into one of her tales. We spent the rest of the afternoon giggling, forgetting for the moment that stories like this were rolling out with the tide.

“Is your internet always this slow?” Mina asked. She stared over my shoulder as I searched the Lumcon website for Dr. Nelson’s email.

I glared at her. “No. Sometimes it doesn’t even work at all.”

“Careful,” Maddie warned. “Jillian takes any complaint against Boutin personally.”

“Of course it’s personal,” I said. “It’s home.”

“Sorry,” said Mina. “I get it. More than once I’ve thought about shoving my little sister into the dishwasher. But nobody else better be mean to her. Last year I thought I was going to have to have a talk with a boy in her class after an eraser incident."

Maddie snorted. I just shook my head. It wasn't the same thing at all.

"Are these the pictures?" she asked.

"Yep." They were still spread across my dresser. Mina peered at them for a long time. "These are really cool," she finally said.

I forgave her for the internet comment.

"Found it!" I said. I copied Dr. Nelson's email address and pasted it into a new email. *Dear Dr. Nelson*, I typed. And then doubt up and made my fingers quit working. She would laugh at me. Or maybe she'd like the idea but think I couldn't pull it off. The curser blinked at me in frustration. My leg started bouncing.

Lucy laid her head on my knee, and it stilled.

I patted her head. "Thanks, girl," I whispered.

I forced my fingers to move. *I am a student at*—my heart squeezed in my chest; I was a Boutin student, but she wouldn't know me from there—*Carolton Middle School*. "I don't know what to say," I finally admitted. I wanted to be sure and brave and tough. What I felt was—inadequate.

"Just tell her about the pictures," Mina said.

"And the stories," Maddie said.

And how everyone needed to know what was happening here, I thought.

I began to type, and between the three of us, we

managed to write the email. I read it all the way through when we were finished, and hope and excitement and fear raced each other in lines just beneath my skin. I was scared she'd say yes, or say no, or maybe ignore me completely. Maddie reached out and put her hand over mine on the mouse. Mina added hers to the top.

We clicked send.

Message sent. We all cheered. And then burst into giggles. Lucy barked and pranced around the room, and we laughed again.

You could always count on friends and dogs.

Chapter Eleven

Hurry up, girl!" Nonnie called from the living room. "I don't want to be walking in with the priest."

We'd never walked in with the priest in our lives. But if Nonnie wasn't fifteen minutes early somewhere, she was late.

I padded into the living room and pulled my rubber boots out of the basket by the door. They were black, not white like the rest of the shrimpers. There was no way I would have shown up in church in shrimp boots—Cajun Reeboks some people called them. But the black didn't look all that bad.

I slid into my raincoat. "I make this look good," I told Mama, who was locating the umbrella.

"You sure do," she said, smiling and pulling my hood up over my head.

Nonnie tucked her pants inside her boots and winked at me. "You get that from my side of the family."

Dad walked into the living room then, wearing jeans

and a nice shirt. We all stopped and stared at him, which made him look extremely uncomfortable.

"Mind if I come to church with you?" he asked.

None of us answered for a moment or two, then Mama rushed to fill the awkward silence. "Of course not."

Nonnie huffed and I shut the door to the hall closet a little too hard.

Dad put on his rain jacket. "Let me just take Lucy out real quick before we go."

I didn't bother telling him I already had. If he'd been paying attention, he would have noticed that Lucy's feet were damp. Damp, not wet, because I had taught her to stand like a statue while I dried her feet.

Water washed over the toe of my boots as I waded across the yard and climbed into the car. Mama sat next to me in the back seat.

"It wouldn't hurt you to be a bit more civil," Mama said, and she had that stubborn set to her chin that meant trouble.

I looked at Mama in surprise. Maybe she thought Dad's going to church was his way of showing up and saying sorry. My mama never talked ugly about my dad, mostly for my sake. But I knew she was mad at him for forgetting me at school. I also knew my mama had more forgiveness than most people. Papa had always said it took a lot of brave for my mama to forgive like she did.

"He's staying in my house," Nonnie said. "I'd

say that's pretty civil. And I let his dog sleep on my furniture."

"Leave Lucy out of this," I said. "She hasn't done anything wrong."

Dad slid into the passenger seat and we stopped talking.

The windshield wipers were on high as Nonnie crept toward town. She had to stop and wait for a car to pass before driving in the left lane around the hole the flood had gouged in the asphalt. Water rushed across the road and filled the hole, and I worried it would only get bigger. There would be no way to get home if this road washed out completely.

The rain became a deluge as we pulled into the church parking lot. There were plenty of open parking spots. The congregation was smaller these days, like all things in Boutin, but it was still the heart of the town.

I stepped into the church and took a deep breath. It smelled like wood polish. The knots in my shoulders loosened. I knew someone a long time ago had built this church, but it felt like it had just grown here, like something out of one of Nonnie's stories. My grandparents had been married in this church. I was baptized here and had taken my first Communion right down there. Every Christmas I helped decorate the tree in the fellowship hall. People changed but the church never did—it stayed solid even when the ground wasn't.

I wasn't the only person rocking rubber boots into

the sanctuary, though some of the older ladies stopped just inside the door to change into nicer shoes. I didn't figure God minded the rubber boots, but I did make sure to wipe them real good.

Maddie and her mom were standing just inside the door. "Good morning, Aunt Susie," I said.

Maddie's mom smiled at me. "Morning, dear." Thunder rumbled overhead, and she looked nervously up at the ceiling. The roof should have been repaired five years ago. "Hope Father Pierre said an extra prayer."

St. Joseph's was lucky our father had the Father's ear, otherwise we'd all have had to be sitting under umbrellas.

Maddie had her iPad and I'd brought paper for anyone who wanted to sign the petition the old-fashioned way.

"We've got about ten minutes," Maddie said.

I didn't waste any time. "Good morning, Mrs. Pitre." I stopped next to the pew where she was sitting. "I was wondering if you would sign the petition to get the school reopened."

She looked at me over the top of her glasses. One small pink curler peeked out from under a mass of gray curls. She'd somehow missed it. "I heard they'd shut the school down for good."

"Yes, ma'am."

"But we can't have a town without a school."

"No, ma'am."

She reached out and took the paper and pen from me, her hand shaking a bit as she signed. "Good luck."

"I was also hoping you might be willing to talk on camera," I said. "We're collecting Boutin stories and I know you have a lot of them."

"I do indeed. You tell your grandma to bring you around some afternoon. I'll tell you as many as you have tape for."

I didn't bother explaining that videos no longer took tapes. "Thanks!"

More and more people trickled into the sanctuary. Dad shook hands with several of his old friends and sent them all my way to sign the petition. I had twelve new signatures before the organ started playing and I had to take my seat. Even the thunderous downpour on the leaky roof midway through the homily couldn't dampen my spirit after that.

After Mass, Father Pierre stood in the hallway and chatted with everyone as they left the sanctuary. The rain had finally slowed to a drizzle, but people were still taking a long time getting outside.

"Nice to see you this morning, Jillian," Father Pierre said when it was my turn to shake his hand. "You're looking very determined."

"Oh, good!" I smiled. "Because I would like you to

sign my petition." I explained again what I was hoping to accomplish at the school board meeting.

"Of course." He took the paper and pen from me and signed his name on an open line. "This is quite a big thing you're doing here."

It felt very big. And sometimes I felt very small. I glanced around at the church, almost as familiar to me as my own house. I imagined it emptying out as people moved away. We just had to get this school reopened. Maybe it would convince the state we were worth saving.

"I'm also collecting Boutin stories. Oral histories. For a project. Would you tell yours?"

"Petitions, projects—you are busy."

"I can't just sit around and do nothing."

"Me neither. I'd be happy to."

A line had formed behind me, so I moved away to let other people talk to Father Pierre. Nonnie and Uncle Pete were standing just outside the front door underneath the overhang.

"Uncle Pete, you'll tell a story on camera, won't you?"

"I've got a great one about a prank your nonnie pulled on Elmer David."

Nonnie stared him down. "If you know what's good for you, you'll pick a different story to tell."

Now I really was dying to hear the story.

"We're leaving church," she said. "You'd think you could behave."

He laughed. "I don't know why you'd think that.

You sure can't. Don't worry, I'll come up with my own story."

"Thanks! Mrs. Pitre and Father Pierre agreed to tell one as well," I told him, more for Nonnie's benefit than his. Maybe that would finally convince her.

"Which one are you telling, Wanda?" Uncle Pete asked, as if he could read my mind.

"I'd better go get the car before the rain starts up again." Nonnie stomped off.

"She doesn't want to talk on camera," I told him.

He watched her go, his face thoughtful. "She takes things hard. Always has."

Maybe that's what I'd inherited from her. "You'll sign the petition to get the school reopened, won't you?"

"Maddie already sent it to me. Aunt Diane and I both signed it."

I squeezed him around the middle. He was squishy and comfortable. "Thanks, Uncle Pete."

I went off to find Maddie. I was hoping she'd gotten even more signatures than I had. I found her talking to Mrs. Anderson.

"You can apply for grants," Maddie was saying. "To help you move."

"I'm too old to move," Mrs. Anderson said.

"But if they'll give you money—"

Maddie was supposed to be helping save our school, not encouraging people to flee. I felt the mad in my face first, but soon it was stomping its way over every square inch of me.

"Not everyone wants to leave as much as you do," I said.

Maddie whirled around, hurt on her face. And a month ago I would have felt bad about that. But in the last month my school had shut down and my town had been condemned by people who thought we weren't important enough to save, and I found that my anger took up so much room that I didn't have any left over for guilt.

"I thought you were getting signatures on the petition," I said.

"I am." She stuck out her chin. "Mrs. Anderson just signed."

"It's hard to have a community without a school," Mrs. Anderson said.

Exactly. I wouldn't let more of Boutin fall away. And Maddie was just helping people leave.

"All my kids went to school here. Got a good education too. I'll text them your petition. They'll sign it."

"Thanks," Maddie said.

"You text?" I asked.

Mrs. Anderson frowned at me. "Don't sound so surprised. Despite my age, I'm not helpless." She tapped on her phone. "There. Operation Reopen Boutin Schools is on its way to Baton Rouge and Houma and Texas."

"Thanks, Mrs. Anderson." I glanced toward the parking lot. Nonnie was probably champing at the bit.

"Jillian!" Dad hollered and waved at me. "Let's go. Your nonnie is champing at the bit."

I huffed. There. That made me sound a little more like Nonnie than my dad.

I wanted to stay to make sure that Maddie didn't talk Mrs. Anderson and half the congregation into moving out of Boutin by next weekend, but I knew how cranky Nonnie could get if she had to wait too long on an empty stomach, so I hustled off after Dad.

"See you tomorrow!" Maddie yelled at my back, but I pretended I was too far away to hear.

I joined Dad. Mud squelched under our boots.

"Nonnie says she's making a redfish court bouillon for lunch. With turnip greens."

I made a face. I loved everything Nonnie made—except turnip greens. And they didn't even go with fish stew. But she was always trying to sneak some green stuff in on me.

Dad laughed. "I hate turnip greens too! Your mama couldn't believe it when I told her after we'd gotten married."

There had probably been plenty more she'd had a hard timing believing. And I didn't care how nasty they tasted—I was going to eat all my turnip greens now.

Dad cleared his throat. "When I get my house fixed, I'd like you to start staying weekends again."

It was a statement, not a question, and I didn't know if this was how he was trying to make up for forgetting me or because he wasn't as busy at work.

And I didn't know exactly what to say about the weekends, so I asked a question instead of giving an answer. "Are you getting close?"

"It's taking longer than I thought. Everyone flooded, so material is on back order and carpenters and floor guys have waiting lists."

I thought about how Dad had sounded when he'd said the word *family* during our poker game. He might have been busy all the time, but I thought he was also really lonely. I had Mama and Nonnie and the entire Boutin community. If my house flooded, I knew at least fifty people who would have shown up.

My dad didn't have anyone. And while that might have been his fault, it still made me feel bad for him. He had missed out on so much.

"Maybe I could help you move in," I said.

"Is this because you want me off the couch quicker?" He smiled to show he was teasing, but he had a little worry crease between his eyebrows.

"Maybe? But mostly it's because I want to help."

The crease between his eyebrows disappeared.

"Do you miss home?" I asked. It was all I thought about these days. How did you know where you stood if everything you used to locate yourself was disappearing?

"It's just a house."

But that wasn't what home was to me. It was all of Boutin—the marshes and trees, the people and traditions. Dad and I were not the same.

"I miss having a bed." He grinned at me. "My back

may never recover from that couch. I think Nonnie stuffs it with rocks when I'm not looking. But I don't miss all the quiet. I like spending time with you."

But would that last? With Dad, I never knew. Just another thing in my life that might disappear.

Chapter Twelve

I heard back from Dr. Evelyn Nelson one week later. I'd gotten into the habit of checking my email every morning before school, holding my breath in hope, exhaling in frustration when I saw the empty inbox. A reply was the first thing I thought about when my eyes popped open.

On Monday I woke up earlier than usual, and too scared to see another empty inbox, or worse, a rejection, I ignored my computer and decided to head outside. Lucy, who just a couple of days ago had abandoned her bed next to the couch to sleep at the foot of my bed, grunted and stretched. In the dark silence, her tail beat a faint good morning on my quilt. It was the nicest way to wake up.

"Good morning, girl," I whispered. Her tail went faster. The sky was just starting to lighten outside my bedroom window. I threw on sweatpants and my rubber boots, wrapped an old blanket around my shoulders, and tiptoed out into the backyard.

It was loud at night, alive with frogs and crickets. Dawn brought the sound of birds and motors—both boat and car. But we were in the pause before the waking, and it was lovely and quiet.

I sat on the bottom step of the porch, and Lucy sank down next to me. The air was damp and cold, and I put my arm around Lucy, bringing her into my side and underneath the blanket. She sat still, and we stared at the horizon as it began to blush pink.

A quiet sort of contentment settled over me. I'd heard a lot of people talk about attending nature's church, and while for some of them it might have been just an excuse to spend Sunday mornings in a boat or deer stand or duck blind, I believed most truly meant it. Watching the sun come up felt like worship.

A lone bird sang out, a sound of pure joy at seeing a new morning, and others soon joined in. Two settled into a small puddle in the yard and bathed themselves.

What a beautiful world we'd been given.

Lucy seemed just as content as I was to watch the morning come. I leaned over and put my cheek on the top of her head. She let it sit there for one breath, then tilted her head up and licked my ear.

I took a deep breath and sent wishes out into the world—that Dr. Nelson would reply, would say yes, that our petition would work, that our town could somehow be saved. An egret coasted across our yard, and I imagined my wish catching a ride on its lacy white wings, soaring closer to heaven than I could manage on my own.

Lucy and I eased back inside, and I heard Nonnie stirring in her room. I fed Lucy and gave her water before heading back to my bedroom.

Dad rolled over on the couch as I went by. "You are so good with her." His voice was still gravelly from sleep, but I thought I heard a little pride and a little regret there.

It made me feel a little of both too.

I checked my email as soon as I got back to my room. I had a reply.

My stomach went to churning like a hurricane in the Gulf, and I took a deep breath and clicked.

Jillian,

I was delighted to receive your email and immediately took your offer to the board of the Wetlands Discovery Center. They were all just as excited as I was and would absolutely make space for the Boutin exhibit. If possible, we would love to unveil the exhibit at our Grand Opening...

I squeaked a little. Read the email again. Closed it, did a little dance across my room, and then stood up tall. The pictures and stories of Boutin would have a home. And I had done that. Me. The girl from a town the state didn't think was worth saving.

"She said yes!" I told Lucy as she trotted into my room to see what all the noise was about. Both of her ears were wet, and she had that little smile on her face. "She said yes." I had to say it out loud a second time to convince myself it was true.

I practically floated into first period.

"Dr. Nelson emailed me back!" I told Maddie and Mina.

Maddie looked stunned. Mina did a little shimmy.

"I'm guessing by your face it was good news?" Maddie asked.

Things had been a bit awkward ever since I overheard Maddie talking about grants. I was still a little mad, and she still wasn't apologizing, but neither of us had mentioned it. So spending time with Maddie was a clumsy little march around the elephant in the room. I hated it. But today hope spread through me like fire through sugarcane.

"The best," I said, and I told them about the grand opening.

Mina leaned back in her chair when I was through, arms crossed. "Wow."

"Yeah, wow," I agreed. "We have a lot of work to do before then."

"And we have to get ready for the school board meeting in two weeks," Maddie reminded me.

"I haven't forgotten." My voice was a little sharper than I wanted. I rounded off the pointy edges. "How's it looking?"

"We've got a lot of signatures," Maddie said.

I knew I needed to use the voice God and the Robichauxs gave me, but Lord I hoped it didn't conk out on me while I was standing in front of all those people. This was important, and I didn't need to go all jittery and trembly, at the meeting or at the grand opening.

"My older brother got a bunch of his friends in high school to sign," Mina said. "Though I had to promise to fold his clothes for a week."

"Thanks." Mina was good people. I hoped there were more like her out there, willing to help even if it didn't directly affect them.

"I hope you're discussing the assignment on the board." Ms. Wilson had ears like a bat and was known to swoop down on students who weren't doing what they were supposed to. Like us.

"We were talking about our petition," I admitted. "Will you sign it?"

Ms. Wilson raised one eyebrow. "You aren't following directions and now you want me to sign a petition?"

My face only got a little red since I knew she was mostly teasing me.

"I enjoy teaching my Boutin students and would

sure miss them if they left, but I've already signed the petition."

I beamed. "You have?"

Ms. Wilson nodded. Maddie looked worried. "Won't you get in trouble with the superintendent?"

"Probably. But I think in this case, it's worth it. Now tell me about your story project."

I blinked. Ms. Wilson smiled. "Dr. Nelson emailed me."

So I told her about Mrs. Labatut's pictures and the stories I was collecting and the bridges falling apart and the grand opening. All that hope I felt kept turning my volume up, so that by the time I was done I was talking too loud and way fast. Mina was taking notes and her pencil was nearly a blur. We had a growing list of people to talk to and places in Boutin to photograph.

"Sounds exciting," Ms. Wilson said before moving on to the next group.

"And I want to plant marsh grass," I said. I wanted to make up for all that time I did nothing. I wanted to do it all now, fix everything I could, use all that mad I'd been feeling to fuel a little change. Maybe even a lot of change. "Dr. Nelson mentioned volunteers when she was here, and I looked it up, and planting starts in March."

"Add it to our list," Maddie said, but Mina was already writing it down.

"Thanks, y'all."

The bell rang and I threw my supplies in my book sack. "Jillian?" Ms. Wilson called out. "A minute?"

The other students filed out of the class and I went and stood in front of Ms. Wilson's desk. It was covered in papers and model atoms and frog food.

"Good luck at the school board meeting, and with the project. What you're doing is so very impressive."

I felt myself go red from the tip-top of my head all the way down to my big toe. "I'm scared." The words just sort of bulldozed their way out. No way of getting them back now.

"I would be too," Ms. Wilson said.

Skeptical walked right across my face. Ms. Wilson smiled. "For true. Talking in front of important people turns my skin all splotchy."

"My mouth forgets how to move and my legs forget how to stop," I admitted. Maybe I could tell Ms. Wilson the truth because I wasn't afraid of disappointing her. She didn't know my people. I didn't have to prove to her that I was more Robichaux than Landry.

"You're doing an important thing," Ms. Wilson said. "Sometimes the scariest steps are the exact ones we need to take."

Maddie and Mina and I spent the next several lunches in the library. Mrs. Landers had editing software on a couple of the computers, and we were working our way through the videos. We'd decided to send those that talked about the school to the superintendent before the meeting. Mina was cutting those into smaller clips.

Maddie and I were making lists of people to visit to get them to sign the petition as well as tell stories. We'd talked to Mrs. Fontenot in English class, and she'd agreed to talk on camera. She'd also signed the petition.

"Do you think the superintendent speaks Cajun French?" Mina asked.

"I doubt it," I answered. "Why?"

"Because I'm pretty sure Mrs. Pitre is swearing in this video."

"At least she remembered to take all her curlers out of her hair," I said.

"I'm really sorry about your school," Mina said. She clicked the mouse and swiveled her chair to look at me. "But I'm glad y'all are here."

I wasn't going to go that far. But I was glad I'd met Mina. You couldn't help but like someone who was that interested in things. "Thanks. For all your help too." *For being my friend*, I thought but didn't want to say out loud. *In a place where I really needed another one.*

"Are you kidding? This is great. We're doing something. A lot of kids laughed at my petition for school lunches. And the one I started to get a recycling program."

"How many petitions have you done?" Maddie asked.

"A lot."

"Have any of them worked?" I asked.

Mina shrugged. "My first one sort of did? In fourth grade the boys wouldn't let the girls play football with them at recess. I started a petition."

"And they let you play?" I asked.

Mina rolled her eyes. "Yeah right."

"So how was that a win?" Maddie asked.

Mina grinned. "I took the petition with all the signatures to the teachers. They said we should start a girls' team. So we did. And then we talked the boys into playing against us and we kicked their butts!"

I burst out laughing, then quickly covered my mouth. Mrs. Landers glanced our way, a slight twist to her mouth. I think she liked Mina's story too.

"You should have come to school in Boutin," Maddie said. "The boys had to let us play because our class is so small."

"Really? You played football? Were you any good?"

It was my turn to shrug. "Maddie never played, but I did all right."

"I don't know if throwing the ball in Derek's face instead of his hands could be considered all right."

"He never stole my lunch again, now did he?"

By the time the bell rang to end lunch, we'd edited another video and added several more people to our list and decided Mrs. Pitre was definitely cussing in her video.

My skin felt tingly and too small, like I might just burst right out of it. This all felt real, possible, exciting.

The number of signatures kept growing. I hadn't quite realized just how much the school meant to people. Before all this, I'd thought of it as my school. But it was ours—all of Boutin's. This town had already lost so much. Land. Funding. We couldn't lose the school too. It was where we gathered, where we took shelter from storms.

Where we learned to write our own stories.

And if we could reopen the school, maybe we could convince the state to fix the roads and bridges. How could they give up on a community that wasn't willing to give up on its home? Surely they couldn't. If we could just win the fight with the school board, maybe we could win one with the state too.

Maybe we could stop people from leaving.

Dr. Nelson said we could make a difference. I wanted to prove it.

"Derek's not right about them not listening to us," I said. "Look at these signatures. People are listening."

"I make it a policy to never actually listen to Derek," Maddie said.

"That's why you're the smartest," I told her.

Mina pushed back from the computer and stretched. "This is going to work."

It had to.

Chapter Thirteen

The Robichauxs and Richards were packed into the small meeting room at the school board office in Carolton. Maddie and I squished together at the end of one row, and Maddie's parents and Mama and Nonnie were in the seats behind us. I hadn't gotten to speak up at the last meeting, and this time, I wanted my voice heard.

"I wonder if this many people always show up at meetings," Maddie whispered.

"This is a normal amount of people," I said, but only to convince myself. If I started thinking about how many people were here, I might not be able to find my voice at all.

"Sorry," Maddie muttered. "Did you know that most people fear public speaking more than, like, plane crashes?"

Maddie and her photographic brain. "Yes, Maddie, right now I actually believe that."

"Again, sorry, I'm just a little nervous too. You're going to do great."

I tried to stare straight ahead, but I couldn't miss the people who kept coming in the door. The Trans and Nguyens came in together. Both were shrimping families, and Mrs. Nguyen was the school secretary. She could tell when a student was actually sick and when what they really needed was a cold drink and a good talk. They were followed by Mr. Champagne, who had been the janitor at Boutin schools since my mom was there. He also cut the grass and shouted the loudest at basketball games and always had butterscotch candies.

"Nervous?" Mina asked. She sat on my other side, camera in hand as she snapped pictures of the audience, the empty table, the flag.

"Terrified?" I pressed my hands against my knees to keep my legs from jittering. It was weird how bouncy my body got when it was supposed to be still. I hoped I could get up enough nerve to speak out. I was terrified that I was just going to sit there, too scared to talk, that I would still be sitting there when everyone left, that I would sit in this chair as they locked the doors and turned out the lights.

I had no problem running my mouth on other occasions. Now I was afraid that it wouldn't start at all.

"Don't think about the people," Mina said. "Think about your school."

I gave her a grateful smile.

All seventeen pages of the petition I'd printed out, plus the ones with actual signatures, were twisted in my sweaty hands. I tried to smooth them out, but my legs were moving too much. Mama put a steady hand on my shoulder.

"You got this," Maddie said.

My legs stilled. I took a deep breath.

The board members and superintendent filed in and sat at two tables at the front of the room. They laughed with one another as they came in, and a few of my raw nerves scooted over to make room for big patches of mad.

They didn't get to be this happy about taking away our school.

"Good evening," Mr. Wright, the superintendent, said. Maddie had tracked down email addresses for the superintendent and all the board members. We'd emailed them the petition and videos, but no one had bothered to respond.

The board talked awhile about the budget. I recounted the number of names on the petition. They talked about some new state rules, and I tried to remember everything I wanted to say.

"The state has approved the continued use of the four temporary buildings outside CHS, the six outside the middle school, and the three outside the elementary school," the superintendent said.

I started paying closer attention.

"The state understands that, for the time being, these temporary buildings will have to become permanent.

Renovations to the existing schools to accommodate the students from Boutin will have to be taken into consideration in the near future."

They would renovate Carolton schools, but not ours. Maybe they figured kids of poor fishermen and laborers should be grateful for whatever they got.

All my mad helped push some of my scared out of the way.

"When are we going to talk about that?" a woman in the back shouted. I turned around. Velma Washington, Mrs. Domingue's granddaughter, was frowning at the board.

The board president leaned into his mic. "That decision was discussed last month."

"It was announced, not discussed," she said.

This time it was the superintendent who spoke. "I know how much Boutin schools mean to your community."

Your, not *our*, because he wasn't from Boutin. He couldn't really understand the traditions, the pride, that would be lost with the school. I took a deep breath and tried to do what Mina said: focus on my school and not the scowling adults sitting at the front of the room.

"This year's flood did tremendous damage to Boutin's already aging school, and in the process of cleanup, workers discovered asbestos."

Ms. Wilson said sometimes we have to take the scary steps. I tried to find all my brave.

"Last year BHS graduated twenty-three students. This year the senior class has twenty members. The kindergarten class is down to twelve."

Maddie's shoulder pressed against mine, and I shifted in my unforgiving seat. It was stifling in here. Someone had turned the heat on to scorch, and everyone breathing at the same time only made it harder for me to catch my own breath. If he didn't get to the point soon, I was liable to suffocate.

"The district doesn't have the money to rebuild a school that, because of fewer people and fewer tax dollars, would have had to close in five years anyway. Carolton schools are newer and safer. There are more extracurriculars available. I wish I had different news, but this decision would not have been made if another solution were possible. I do believe that it will be one that will benefit everyone involved."

"It's still dark when my child gets on the bus. How is that beneficial?"

Other voices joined in until no one was listening to anyone else.

I wiped my hands on my jeans. My mouth was dry as I glanced back at Mama and Nonnie. Mama smiled encouragingly, and Nonnie gave me a curt nod. I stood up. "I would like to speak."

My voice wasn't much more than a squeak. People kept talking. I stepped out into the aisle, and it got a little quieter. I pushed all my brave toward my mouth.

"I have something to say."

It got quiet enough that I was pretty sure everyone could hear my heart hammering.

"My name is Jillian Robichaux."

"You are not on the agenda," one of the board members said.

Nonnie hissed and Mama looked like she was about to climb over the chairs, but Maddie was the one who stood up and spoke. "This is a public meeting. The public is allowed to speak. And I think students should get a say."

I was going to hug Maddie so hard later.

"Let her talk," the superintendent said.

Maddie sat down.

"When I think of home, I think of the rosebushes each graduating class plants around the school. I think of crawfish boils and potlucks down at the church and sitting with my grandparents in the boat, listening to their stories while I prayed I'd get a bite on my line. Home is comforting and familiar and personal.

"So you can't close our school. You can't take away something that familiar and personal to this community." I paced the aisle and stopped worrying that people would notice my unsteady hands and the shake in my voice. "My parents went to Boutin. My grandparents. Their parents. If you close our school, I'll be the first person in my family not to graduate from Boutin High."

I'd heard so many stories about school traditions over

the years, and I couldn't believe that I might not get to participate in any of them, might not get to make stories of my own.

"Families with kids want to live close to good schools. If you close our school, people will leave faster than they already are, and new families won't move in. And what would Boutin be without families? They say we're going underwater, that fixing our roads and bridges isn't a priority, and I know the school board can't save the whole town. But keeping Boutin schools open for as long as possible will help us get to stay. Our school might be small, but that doesn't mean it isn't important to us. Boutin still has plenty of children, and we want to learn."

And we wanted to learn surrounded by our community.

"Mrs. Hebert taught my mom math, but now she's in Baton Rouge because after thirty years at Boutin Middle, she lost her job. Ms. Pam in the cafeteria slipped extra rolls to hungry kids. The teachers at Carolton are nice, but they aren't family. The Carolton school is nice, but it isn't home."

Someone in the back started clapping. Then almost everyone joined in. I stopped pacing and looked around me. I'd almost forgotten I had an audience. Nonnie was smiling and Mama was crying and Maddie gave me a thumbs-up. Mina snapped my picture.

My voice hadn't given out after all. And people had actually listened to me.

The board president whacked his gavel on the table. It got quiet again.

The superintendent leaned forward. "I believe it's important for our students to get a chance to speak. So I thank you for that."

Well, not everyone had listened. I could see his answer in his face. I held up my swampy paper. "I have a petition with 1,327 signatures. We emailed you a copy."

He chuckled. "They certainly are doing a good job teaching civics." His smile said I was a child and he'd heard enough.

Well, I was a child, and I'd *had* enough. Mama and Nonnie had always told me I could do anything, but that wasn't really true. I was only one person. I didn't make this mess. People older than me had used up the land until it didn't have any more to give, and instead of fighting for it, they moved on somewhere else.

And we were left with nothing.

"This was a tragic and unforeseen occurrence. We are unable to hold school in the destroyed buildings. Carolton was gracious enough to open its doors to those displaced students. In the long run, this decision will save money and allow us to better serve our students. Our decision to close Boutin schools was approved and signed by the BESE board. You are welcome to see it for yourself at the conclusion of this meeting. For now, we will continue to do the best we can in a difficult situation."

And that was it. The board concluded their business and the meeting adjourned with the sharp strike of a gavel.

I stood in the aisle as people flowed around me. Strangers said nice things, but all I heard was no. *No, the petition didn't work. No, we won't repair the building.*

No, Boutin schools will not reopen.

"You did so well."

I looked up. Ms. Wilson was standing in front of me.

"But it didn't matter."

Ms. Wilson put her hands on my shoulders. "Of course it mattered."

I didn't want a lesson on speaking up or trying my best. I'd done both. What I wanted was a different outcome. What I wanted was for those outside Boutin to care.

What I'd wanted was to be heard.

"You must be her mother," Ms. Wilson said.

Mama had appeared, her face both smiles and tears. "A proud one at that."

I had to get out of that room. I mumbled something about finding Maddie and Mina and pushed my way outside. I walked away from the building, past the crowd still milling outside, and steadied myself against an oak tree. My nerves were gone, but so was some of my anger, which left plenty of room for my sad.

Maddie found me. "We tried."

"And failed."

"But you did great!" Mina said.

"I need everyone to quit saying that!" Great would have been them agreeing to save our school. This was the very most opposite of great. It felt like I was drowning, and I kept waving and shouting, and everyone just smiled and waved back, not even noticing that anything was wrong.

Yes, it was good that I'd said what I'd wanted to. But that didn't mean anything if it hadn't made any difference.

I just wanted to scream. Maybe they'd pay attention to that.

"Jillian Robichaux?" I didn't know the woman who said my name. She wore jeans and a blazer and was one of the first people all night who didn't look at me like I was some stupid kid trying to play grown-up.

"Yes?"

"My name is Isa Garcia. I'm with the Carolton paper. Could I ask you a few questions?"

My heart was sore and all I wanted to do was go home. I thought I was all talked out. But then I thought about all the people who had no idea what was going on, who might help if they only had a little more information. I thought about the fact that my entire town was sinking underwater and I hadn't really known anything about it.

"Okay."

Because I still had a lot to say.

Chapter Fourteen

You're a celebrity," Mina said, staring at the newspaper sitting on my desk. Isa Garcia had run my story and picture in the Carolton paper.

"Hardly," I muttered. I was some kind of embarrassed that my face was printed big on the page, but I was not ashamed of talking about what was happening in Boutin. People needed to know.

Maddie, Mina, and I were editing videos, making a list of places to photograph, and taking turns rubbing Lucy's belly. She was lying on her back, all four legs in the air, tongue hanging out of her mouth.

"I gotta get out of this house," Nonnie announced as she came into my room. She'd been cooking all morning for Mary Delapasse, whose foot had taken a nasty turn. Apparently her sister wasn't a saint after all. I was pretty sure most everyone in Boutin could have told her that—and probably had. Nonnie glanced at Lucy and rolled her eyes, but she didn't even bother hiding her smile. Nonnie was all soft spot, when you got right down to it. "Grab your coats."

"You aren't going to make us go with you to Mrs. Delapasse's, are you?" I grimaced. I did not want to have to look at that foot.

"No, your mama is taking the food over there."

Because if anyone was a saint, it was my mama. She was all bravery and kindness. And you had to have both to spend the afternoon with Mary Delapasse and her rotting foot.

"I have an envie for shrimp boulettes, and we're all out of shrimp."

I jumped out of my chair so fast that I scared Lucy. She rolled over and bounded to her feet, looking for the threat. I patted her head. "Want to ride in the boat?" I asked her.

Her tail swished back and forth. She might not have understood everything I said, but she had mastered the word *want*. And she always wanted.

"Y'all up for some cast netting?" Nonnie asked Maddie and Mina. She never had to ask me. I was always up for it.

They were both already grabbing their coats. It wasn't that cold outside—sixty-five degrees or so probably—but for my Louisiana blood, that was chilly. It would be even cooler on the water.

Dad had gone to work on his house this morning. I'd pretended to be asleep when he'd eased open the door and asked Lucy if she'd wanted to go for a ride. She'd wagged her tail but stayed curled up at the end of the bed. She'd probably just been too cozy to move, but it had felt like she'd picked me. I'd snuggled into my covers and gone right back to sleep.

I'd been upset and unsettled all week, mad at the school board, mad at myself, just mostly mad. I needed out of the house just as bad as Nonnie did.

"Bring home lots of shrimp!" Mama said from the front porch as we climbed into Papa's old truck. Nonnie had the boat trailer already hooked on.

I scooted in next to Nonnie. Maddie and Mina came next, and Lucy managed to squeeze onto the floorboard, her head perched on Mina's knee.

"That dog can ride in the bed," Nonnie grumbled as she started the truck.

"As if. That's not safe." Besides, Lucy was family now.

Nonnie glanced at the four of us crammed together. "This probably isn't much safer."

It was a short ride to the boat launch. Maddie and I pointed out Boutin points of interest to Mina as we passed: Dell's Grocery, the trailer that had washed up in Mr. Wayne's backyard after the last hurricane and been left to rust (though he did use it as a storage room now).

"And this is where the road washed away after the flood," I said as Nonnie eased around the gaping hole. "Guess they won't be fixing that."

"Pretty sure they don't fix the roads in Baton Rouge either," Nonnie muttered.

The great part about launching the bateau was that I

got to drive Papa's truck. Nonnie backed the boat trailer in, put the truck in park, and got in the boat. I slid over into the driver's seat. Mina looked a little nervous.

"I do this all the time," I told her. And by all the time, I meant twice.

Nonnie eased the boat off the trailer, and when she was clear, I put the truck in drive. Papa's truck was old and loud and reliable, and it gave a little lurch as it fell into gear. I pressed on the gas slow, sat up tall to see over the steering wheel, and rolled forward, parking at the edge of the grass. I had to yank on the gear shift a bit to get it to slide into park, but I finally found it.

"Not bad," Mina admitted. "My mom won't let me start practicing driving yet."

"Could you even see over the dash?" Maddie asked.

"Hey now!" Mina protested as she hopped out of the truck. She had a short little fall before she found the ground. She grinned over her shoulder. "Fine. Probably not."

"I don't really think that counts as driving," Maddie said as we walked to the boat. "We coasted a few yards. More like parking."

"It counts," I assured her.

"Do you know that some adults in big cities don't even know how to drive?" Maddie asked. She climbed in the boat. "They don't need to know how. They can just take a cab or bus or the subway." Her face lit up a little. "Or a train."

"Maddie's always wanted to ride on a train," I told Mina.

Mina looked a little wistful. "That would be so cool. I've only flown on a plane once."

"You have?" Maddie looked impressed and jealous and maybe a little sad.

"I was eight," Mina said as she got in the boat, "and I threw up."

Lucy leapt in after Mina, and when I was sure everyone was seated, I pushed us off and jumped in. "Well, I prefer boats."

I secured Lucy's life jacket as Nonnie eased away from the bank. She sped up, and I burrowed into my coat, eyes watering.

Maddie huddled down in the boat to try and stay warm. Mina pulled her hood on but sat up straight and watched the marsh pass by. I kept my arm around Lucy and felt myself unspool.

I didn't know how Maddie, how anyone, could walk away from this. Maybe we didn't have trains and museums and fancy restaurants and clothing stores. But I thought what we did have made up for what we didn't.

We had wide-open sky. It was a typical winter day—the haze we normally had due to the thick air was gone, leaving us sitting under a cloudless, deep-blue ceiling. The chilly air nipped at my cheeks as Nonnie went faster.

We had water and marsh grass, egrets and a peace that came with the space to spread out. We were headed out to catch dinner—me, my nonnie, my friends, and my dog.

It didn't get any better than that.

Nonnie finally decided on a spot and shut off the boat. The water was shallow here, perfect for the cast nets. We had to be careful not to tangle each other. Nonnie sat at the back of the boat and let us do the catching. I tossed my net out and began dragging it in, the weights closing around what I hoped was shrimp. Lucy leaned eagerly over the side of the boat, panting, tongue lolling, eyes following every jerk of the net. I pulled the net up, then dropped it in a five-gallon bucket and yanked the string to open it.

Several large shrimp plopped into the bucket. Nonnie leaned over, frowning, judging.

"Not a bad size," she finally declared.

I felt a little taller as I threw the net again.

Nonnie had brought us each a bucket, and Maddie and Mina soon had theirs each about half full. We complimented each other on the shrimp, giggled at the tiny fish we snagged and had to toss back into the water, but mostly we were quiet, our ears filled with the sound of wind and water.

When we caught our limit, we headed back. Lucy, who'd stuck her head in each bucket several times, had finally gotten bored and fallen asleep in the bottom of the boat.

"We've got to give Mina the full experience," Nonnie

said as she navigated out of the marsh. The wind rippled the water and bowed the grass.

"What's the full experience?" Mina asked.

I grinned. "The Shrimp Shed," Maddie and I said at the same time.

"We're not selling these though, right?" I asked.

"Nope. What doesn't make it into tonight's dinner is going in the freezer."

Summer was a slog through heat and humidity, but Louisiana winters were mild, and even though the wind was chilly, the sun kept it from being cold enough to drive people inside. Despite, or maybe because of, the news that the Shrimp Shed was closing, plenty of people were gathered, both outside and in. Some of the old-timers were drinking coffee in small Styrofoam cups. Everyone was sharing news and the occasional gossip.

They folded us into their group when we walked up.

"Can't believe they've shut the school down," Mr. Naquin said. He wore a ragged United Houma Nation baseball cap, and his jeans and LSU T-shirt had paint splatters on them. "My grandpa helped build it, even though his kids couldn't go. I was the first one in my family to graduate from there."

"Your grandpa must have been proud," Mina said.

"He was. He was big on education. All my younger siblings graduated after I did." The smile slid from his weathered face and he shook his head. "Boutin was always so proud of its school. What a shame."

"Mr. Naquin," I said, pulling out my cell phone, "would you mind telling that story on camera?"

It turned out he didn't mind at all.

Nonnie had been right—Bud Talbot sure was a talker. He'd sidled up to listen to Mr. Naquin's story and couldn't wait to tell his own.

"Did you know I grew up next door to your grandpa?" he asked me.

"No." Most days it was hard to imagine that Nonnie and Papa lived an entire lifetime before I came along.

"We used to duck hunt together. We used live decoys." His eyes danced a Cajun two-step.

"I've never heard of that," I said.

"Because it's illegal as heck," one of the men shouted, and they all laughed. A crowd had gathered. Sit long enough outside the Shrimp Shed and you could visit with almost everyone in town. I wondered where everyone would gather once this was gone. Would Mr. Willie board the place up or just let it sit? I couldn't imagine anyone buying it. New businesses were not coming to Boutin. Besides, I couldn't imagine anything else filling this building.

"We fed the ducks table scraps to save money, but it makes their feathers greasy and they sink, so once duck season rolled around, we'd save up our money and feed them corn. But one year, the night before opening day of season, I snuck over to his house and fed all his ducks scraps. The next morning, when we went out and put them on the water, all his floated low in the water. Only their necks stuck up." Bud laughed until tears squirted from his eyes. "Oh, he was mad at me about that."

"I bet he got you back," I said. Papa always had been good for a prank.

Bud wiped his face. "He sure did. He stole my high school sweetheart while I was off building the pipeline."

"Are you talking about my nonnie?"

"I sure am."

It was even harder to believe Nonnie'd had a lifetime before Papa. They'd laughed and bickered and teased and grumped for over forty years. I glanced over at her. She seemed to be arguing with Willie Guidry. "Mr. Bud, I think you might have dodged a bullet there."

"I think you're right."

"You worked on the pipeline?" Maddie asked.

"Sure did. One of the few steady jobs down here. I know it's the thing right now to talk ugly about the oil industry, and they took us for granted, no doubt, but they fed us for a long time. In the twenties, the timber industry wiped out so much of our landscape, but they also gave people jobs and food and hope. The oil companies did the same thing. Fishing and shrimping is a fickle way to earn a living. Sometimes the catch is good and sometimes it isn't, but the bills roll in no matter what. You do what needs to be done for your family and you don't feel shame in that."

Mina held up her phone. "Tell us about that." So he did.

Patty Cannatella talked about her family's bakery.

They went to work in the middle of the night baking breads and pastries. That's how she met her husband. He'd stop in on his way home from work in the mornings and get a loaf of French bread for his mama and one to eat on the way. "Downtown always smelled like fresh-baked bread," she said.

"Boy I miss that," said Mr. Naquin. The bakery had shut down fifteen years ago.

"Me too." Ms. Patty's voice held sorrow and humor both, a note I'd discovered in Nonnie's voice, too, after Papa died. A widow's melody. Patty had lost her husband soon after the BP oil spill. They'd gone out fishing one afternoon and he'd died three days later from a flesh-eating bacteria BP said had nothing to do with the stuff they put in the water to eat the oil.

Ms. Fran was the oldest lady here, the joints of her hands swollen with arthritis, her hair gone completely white. But she kept it long and braided in a thick plait down her curved back.

"When I was seventeen years old, I snuck out my bedroom window in the middle of the night and me and my girlfriends drove all the way to Shreveport to see Elvis Presley at the Louisiana Hayride."

"You did not," Ms. Patty said.

Ms. Fran looked like the cat who ate the canary. "I did."

"You actually saw Elvis Presley?" Maddie asked.

"I did. And it only cost sixty cents to get in."

Mina was filming, so I just stood there with my mouth open. Elvis Presley was kind of a big deal back in the day.

"I bet it cost a whole lot more than that when you got home," Ms. Patty said.

Ms. Fran laughed, and for a minute, I could almost picture her as a teenager, pink-cheeked and smiling, her thick hair blowing in the wind as she sang along to the radio and roared up Highway 1.

The people standing here had gone to school together, buried loved ones together, survived floods and growing families and lean years together. Every person here was connected in some way, by a tiny thread or by dozens, and it was comforting to be part of such an intricate tapestry.

"I thought I heard trouble brewing."

I swung around to find my dad strolling toward us like he belonged here. Lucy trotted to his side, and he patted her head and joined the crowd.

"Bobby Landry, how are you, pod'na?" Mr. Bud asked.

"Upright," Dad answered.

"For now," someone added, and the crowd laughed.

It was strange standing outside the Shrimp Shed with my dad. The people in this crowd were there for me and my mom when Dad wasn't. Mr. Willie and his wife, Janelle, had brought over more food than anyone could eat after Papa died. Mr. Naquin had stopped and helped

Mama fix a flat once when he'd passed her coming back from Carolton. Above all, they were consistently here, dependable, unchanging when everything else had changed. A community like that makes a person feel safe.

"Has your daddy ever told you the story about the time his daddy had a run-in with Lydie Thibault?"

I shook my head. I didn't know any of the Landry stories. He'd never taken the time to tell me.

Dad didn't need any more prodding than that. He launched into his story. "My dad fished and shrimped like most everyone else down here, and when that wasn't enough, he took on odd jobs, painting houses, fixing roofs, things like that."

I'd never known my grandparents on that side. Grandpa Landry had died before I was born, and Grandma Landry had died when I was three. I didn't remember her. My dad had two brothers who were a lot older than him, and they'd both moved out of state when my dad was still a kid. I didn't know either of them.

"Lydie Thibault had hired my dad to repaint her house. I was twelve or so at the time, and helping him when I could. 'I'm going to have to charge you extra,' he'd told Lydie Thibault after he'd inspected the place. 'Whoever painted the last time must have been in a hurry to take your money. The windows have been painted shut.'

"Mrs. Thibault had swelled up like a toad then. 'Blast it, Three-or-Four Landry!' she'd hollered. My dad's name was Theodore," he explained to me, "and you knew you were in trouble if Mrs. Thibault got your name wrong. '*You* painted the house the last time!'"

I'd almost forgotten we were surrounded by people until they started laughing. I joined in, and in that moment, it didn't feel weird to have Dad sharing stories alongside everyone else. It felt like he belonged there.

It wasn't an entirely unpleasant feeling.

"'I plumb forgot!' he'd always tell me. And he didn't end up charging her extra after all."

"I bet not!" Ms. Fran said. "You didn't mess with Lydie Thibault!"

Nonnie was leaning against one of the front porch posts, listening but keeping her distance from the crowd. That wasn't like Nonnie, but I thought I knew why.

Mr. Willie Guidry told his story last. Most of the crowd had trickled away, fond smiles on their faces as they headed off to their dinners. Dad had taken Lucy home, and Nonnie was waiting on us in the truck.

"The Blessing of the Fleet used to be my favorite day," Mr. Willie said. "Right up there with Christmas."

We still had the Boat Blessing every spring, but Nonnie said it just wasn't the same as it had been. More and more it felt like I'd been born too late, missed out on so many good things.

"People came from all over to participate. You

couldn't get a seat at Mass—we were jammed in like sardines. Then the priest and altar boys would lead us all out to the boats. The priest would climb into the lead boat. You can't imagine the decorations. Brightly colored flags fluttered in the spring breeze, and everyone was happy, laughing and excited, about the party to come, about the season to come, about the year to come. There was a lot of hope back then."

Plenty of us still had hope. It was just harder to find. But I sure wasn't going to stop looking.

"Then we'd have the boat parade—boats as far as the eye could see! More than two hundred boats to be sure. They say Lafitte sailed up this bayou."

I'd heard that story more than once. Only Louisiana would raise the pirate Jean Lafitte to hero status. I mean, he did save New Orleans. But he also did a heap of horrible things. We liked our scoundrels.

"Plenty of people without boats would drive down here just to see the parade. They'd bring picnic lunches and lawn chairs and wave and cheer as we passed. Then we'd anchor, and the party started. Families climbed on board and we'd eat and dance."

Papa had loved to dance. Sometimes he'd turn on music and grab Nonnie up. She'd grumble and fuss, but the minute they started dancing, she'd start smiling and laughing. Papa could do that to her. Dancing could too.

I wanted to see Boutin dancing again.

"We've held on to a lot of traditions over the years,"

said Mr. Willie, "but this is one of them that is fading away. Pretty soon, it will be gone completely."

"That's why we're recording these stories," I said.

He smiled, but it was a sad smile. "You're doing a good thing, Jillie. But telling about these stories sure isn't the same as living them. I wish for your sake that we'd done a better job of saving some of this."

So did I. But Nonnie always said wish in one hand and spit in another and see which one filled faster. I could wish all I wanted—I just had to do something as well. This was part of the doing.

Mr. Willie sat on the bench outside his business, the faded boards behind him. I stood in front of him with my phone, and Maddie and Mina sat on the worn boards of the deck, legs crisscrossed as they listened.

"My grandfather started the Shrimp Shed. I never thought I'd be the one to let it go."

"But you don't have to! Nonnie says those people can't come down here and tell us what to do."

"That's what she was just telling me," Mr. Willie said, but I could tell from his face her words hadn't been as polite. "They aren't, not really. Them not fixing the bridges is bad, but they can't stop the water rising. They can't stop the land crumbling away. It's too late."

I didn't want to believe that. I couldn't believe that. "But you don't have to leave now. There's still some time."

"The marina over in Grand Isle is newer. Bigger.

There are condos and camps for rent over that way. Tourists don't come here to shrimp, and there aren't enough shrimpers here anymore to pay my bills. People were leaving Boutin long before the state's announcement. There just aren't that many jobs here. I love this place, but I can also want better for my kids and grandkids, just like everyone else."

I didn't see how anywhere could be better than Boutin.

Mama said people from Boutin were resilient. Nonnie used the word *stubborn*. But lately there was too much giving up going on around here. The state had decided we weren't worth saving. They didn't care about a community that had lived here and fished here and laughed and loved and cried here for generations. We no longer fit into their box.

As people moved on, this culture would die. It had shrunk considerably over the years, but as families moved and stopped living off the land, stopped fishing and shrimping, stopped blessing the boats and telling stories and sharing food, their children and then their children would grow further away from this life. They'd adopt the life of Applebee's and the Gap, a life that looked the same no matter where you lived it.

I didn't want that. When I imagined my life as a grown-up, I saw myself here like all the Robichauxs before me. I wanted my own boat. I wanted a porch swing with a view of the marsh and the sunset. I wanted to always fall asleep to the sound of frogs and wake to birdsong. I did not want traffic noise and neighbor noise and concrete.

I wanted so many things that sometimes it felt like I'd be consumed with the wanting.

And some of that wanting was for things not to change at all. I wanted the good parts of Boutin to stay the same, to be perfectly preserved like some insect in amber, a portrait of a way of life that didn't need to disappear.

Because without all those things, I was afraid I had no idea who I was.

Chapter Fifteen

The holidays kept everyone busy, so it wasn't until January that we started working hard on editing the videos we'd recorded down at the Shrimp Shed. It made me feel like I was doing something at least, given I'd failed at getting what I'd wanted at the school board meeting last month.

"Your dad seems nice," Mina said. She'd called to ask a question about the video she'd recorded of my dad's story. I still hadn't decided if I was going to include it in our project. These stories were about Boutin, and he didn't live here anymore. Not really.

Lucy gave a little snore. She had her head resting on my foot, so I couldn't move even if I'd wanted to. And I didn't.

"He is nice." That was part of the problem. He was funny and charming and helpful. He was a hard worker and a good neighbor. Everyone said lovely things about him, which usually made me feel worse, because I hadn't had many opportunities to see that version in action.

Boutin's stories were revealing plenty that I hadn't known. Until I'd found those pictures and heard Mrs. Anderson's story about Cooper's Dock, I hadn't fully understood what was happening to Boutin. And I'd thought I'd known pretty much all there was to know about my dad, until Mrs. Millie's story showed me that wasn't completely true.

I wanted to believe that stories healed.

A text from Maddie came through.

Fiddler's Point!

I'll add it to the list, I texted back.

We were making a list of drowned places to photograph for our project. Nonnie had promised to take us around to get the pictures.

"Dinner!" Nonnie shouted. Lucy immediately woke up.

"I got to go," I said.

"See you tomorrow!" Mina hung up.

I stood up and stretched. Lucy jumped off my bed and did the same, yawning wide.

"Just the seasoning this chicken needs," Nonnie said when we walked into the kitchen. "Dog hair."

"Don't listen to her," I said, patting Lucy. "We all know she spoils you rotten when no one is looking."

"All bark and no bite," Dad said.

Nonnie glared at him. "I wouldn't test that theory if I were you."

"Now children," Mama said. She looked like she

could have used some Lucy snuggles. Her smile was only half as bright, like it wasn't fully charged up, and that meant she was worried. I wrapped my arms around her waist and gave her a little squeeze.

She squeezed back. "Thanks. I needed that."

Me too.

We fixed our plates and sat at the table. Nonnie had quit banishing Lucy from the kitchen, so she laid at my feet and looked ever hopeful that I'd drop something.

We'd all become messy eaters since Lucy showed up.

"The Discovery Center is giving us a whole wall for our Boutin project," I said. Dr. Nelson had sent me a picture. Seeing all that blank space that we were supposed to fill with pictures and stories made my insides squirm. Doing this project was one thing—sharing it with the world was something else. It had to be good.

Because it mattered.

"That's so great," Mama said, but half of her sounded like it was somewhere else.

"Already more accomplished than anyone else in your family." Nonnie winked at me.

I took advantage of her good mood to try again. "I can't imagine not having one of your stories be a part of it. Please?"

She stilled, all traces of good mood wiped clean off. "I don't want some video camera stuck in my face while I talk about what it's like to see my hometown disappear." Nonnie fussed and stewed and roared often. But she was rarely ever truly angry. Right now, she was mad. And sad. Her face softened, and she leaned closer to me to whisper. "I'm sorry, cher. It's too close."

I nodded. I understood. Mostly.

We ate in uncomfortable silence after that. Until Mama finally sighed and spoke the words that must have been causing her all the worry she'd been wearing. "I think we should move."

My fork clattered against my plate. Nonnie continued chewing, pretending Mama hadn't said a word.

"I love this place as much as either of you, but we've got to be practical. No doctors. No road repairs. And now no school. They'll shut the phones off, then the electricity and gas. Then what?"

"They'd really turn off the power? With people still living here?"

"They won't do any such thing," Nonnie assured me.

"Fact is, they aren't repairing that bridge," Dad said. "It could go at any moment."

I pictured the bridge collapsing just as we drove over it. I felt myself going turtle, my shoulders inching up toward my ears, the rest of me wishing for a hard shell to protect me. Mama cut her eyes at Dad in warning.

"It could not," Nonnie said, her jaw set. "That bridge will probably outlast all of us. I'm not moving away because some kid in the state office said it might happen."

"I know a man who works for DOTD," Dad said. "He agrees it's in pretty bad shape."

"You stay out of this," Nonnie snapped. "You have absolutely no say about any part of our lives."

A flush bloomed from just underneath the collar of Dad's shirt and raced upward, but he didn't say anything.

I didn't either. I couldn't untangle a single word from the jumble of pleas and arguments that were knotted up inside my head.

"I'm not leaving the house I've lived in for over forty years."

I'd lived in this house half my life. I wasn't leaving either.

"Mom." My mama sounded more serious than I'd heard her in a long time. "We can't stop what's happening, but it is happening. And we need to be somewhere safer, where there are doctors. Ruth Ann Babin died last week waiting for an ambulance."

"Ruth Ann Babin had a massive heart attack. She could have been living inside the hospital and it wouldn't have made any difference."

I bounced my right leg and tore my roll into little pieces. Any bravery I had was long gone. I felt fear and dread. This really couldn't be happening. Robichauxs didn't run.

"We need to be where the roads aren't crumbling and the water actually recedes after a rain. And we need to get there before it's too late."

"Then you go." Nonnie pushed her plate away. "But I'm staying."

"No!" Lucy jumped, startled at my shout. "We're a family and we stay that way." We were already smaller than we used to be. I would not let this separate us. We were stronger together.

"Wanda, I know you don't want to hear this, especially from me, but you aren't getting any younger, and you will need to be closer to doctors. Nora shouldn't have to drive so far to work."

I'd never have believed that my parents would be on the same side of anything.

"You haven't ever thought about what Nora needed before, so don't start now." Nonnie's voice had a quiet rumble of anger in it, like thunder getting closer. My skin felt all prickly and hot. "This is the last time I'm going to tell you to stay out of it. Nora is a grown woman and can do exactly what she wants. But so can I. And I'm not giving up on my home."

No one was eating anymore. Lucy had escaped to the living room.

"Leaving Boutin isn't giving up," Mama said. "It's just moving to higher ground."

"You'll have to bury me first."

"That's exactly what I'm afraid of!" The words burst out of Mama and forced me out of my chair. My napkin fell on the floor but I left it.

"Stop," I said, even while I didn't. No one listened to me. I paced from one end of the kitchen to the other.

Mama took a deep breath. "And where would I bury you? The cemetery is underwater."

"Then throw me in the bayou next to your daddy, because I'm not going anywhere else." She got to her feet. "No one's dying. Stop scaring Jillian."

Nonnie whirled on her heel and stomped outside.

I wandered to the other side of the kitchen like an unmoored ship in the center of a hurricane.

"Thibodaux is nice," Dad said, like this was still a normal conversation we were having. "Good schools, a college. And I would be closer to Jillian."

"We're moving to Carolton," Mama said. "I work there. Jillian goes to school there."

I pounded my fist on the kitchen counter and Mama finally looked at me. "We're not moving at all! You didn't raise me to run when things got hard. You taught me to fight for what matters. And Boutin matters."

It mattered more than anything.

Mama got up and came toward me, but I did not want a hug. She stopped and stood in the center of the kitchen. "I know, baby, but you can't fight Mother Nature."

I wanted to scream *Traitor*, to shout that she couldn't abandon Nonnie and me and Boutin, our entire lives, but my anger and sorrow had swelled into a leaden balloon and no words could find their way around it. The backs of my eyes burned.

"Jillian, it's time to grow up," Dad said. "This isn't a fight you can win."

Grow up? I'd gone through a flood, lost my school.

My favorite place in the whole world was disappearing right from under my feet, and my dad thought I was being immature just because I was upset?

My dad didn't fight for family. He just ran.

I grabbed on to my anger with both hands. It felt a lot easier and safer than despair.

"You don't get a say in our lives," I told him. "You left. We stayed."

He stared at me in disbelief for a moment, and when no one said anything, he whirled on Mama. "Are you going to let her talk to me like that?"

"I'm not her only parent," Mama said. She was holding her arms tight around her middle.

"Things were fine until you got here," I said. Mama had never once mentioned moving until Dad mentioned it first. He put the idea in her head. He was the one who left when things were hard. We didn't.

"Do you want me to leave?"

I'd spent a long time wanting him here, wishing he'd want us. But now? "I just want everything to go back to the way it was before."

"Then I'll go," he said.

Because of course he'd rather leave than deal with the hard stuff. Everyone around me was leaving. I let my anger propel me right out of the room, out of the house. Lucy didn't follow this time.

Chapter Sixteen

Dad was true to his word—for once in his life. When I woke up the next morning, he wasn't on the sofa. His clothes weren't spilling out of boxes in the hallway. I didn't have to wait until he was out of the shower to brush my teeth.

He hadn't even said goodbye.

Guilt stole my appetite. Losing my temper with Dad had been partly his fault and partly because it felt good to blame someone for something that was both no one and everyone's fault.

Mama and Nonnie were barely speaking. A cuddle from Lucy would have made me feel a little better, but Lucy was gone.

Nonnie didn't try and make me talk, but she gave me an extra-long hug before I left for school. The horizon tinged the prettiest shade of blush as Mama and I pulled out of the driveway. Boats, both old and new, lined the canal off to our left, with names like *Anna Marie* and *Linda Ann* and *Mia Maloy*.

The world was beautiful to look at but hard to live in sometimes.

"I know you're upset," Mama said.

Upset did not have enough bells and whistles to adequately describe how I was feeling. Betrayed, hurt, sad, angry—if there was a word that meant all of those things at once, then that was what I was. "Are you going to tell me you were joking about the whole moving thing?"

"No."

"Then I don't want to talk about it right now." I could not sit still in this car and listen to Mama talk about moving away from home, away from Nonnie.

I waited for Mama to fuss me for getting sassy with her, with Dad last night, but she only looked sad, nodded once, and turned back to the road. We didn't talk the rest of the way to school.

I managed to make it to lunch without talking much to anyone—my scowl was obviously fully functioning. The tables in the cafeteria were no longer carefully guarded territories—Carolton and Boutin students mixed together almost as if we'd never been two different schools. Eventually people would forget we ever had been. I grabbed my tray and took it out to the courtyard so I could be alone.

But Maddie and Mina found me anyway.

"We left you alone all morning," Maddie said. "And if you don't want to talk, you don't have to."

"But we're sitting with you." Mina slid her tray next to mine.

I didn't want company. I wanted to glare at my food and stew in silence. But the words pushed their way out anyway. "My dad left."

"Why?" Mina asked.

Maddie didn't bother asking. She'd been there all the times he hadn't shown. She knew he didn't really need a reason.

"Because I kind of told him to." I picked at my spaghetti. "My mom wants to move." I expected gasps and shouts of horror, all my anger and shock on their faces. I didn't get any of that. "Did you hear me?"

"My parents have been talking about it too," Maddie said.

"Why didn't you tell me?" We were supposed to tell each other everything.

"Because it's just talk right now. After the state's announcement, I'm pretty sure everyone is talking about it."

"Nonnie's not going to leave," I said.

"No, Aunt Nonnie won't be going anywhere."

"Then we shouldn't either!" I didn't want to leave Nonnie behind. I didn't want to leave at all.

"What are your other options?" Mina asked.

"I don't have any options. I'm thirteen years old, and I have to do what my mother says, no matter how much I hate it. You don't understand. You aren't losing your home."

Her eyes narrowed but she didn't say anything.

"And you hate Boutin anyway," I told Maddie. I was tired of cramming my anger into tiny spaces. I wanted to let it out, to scream and rage at the world. "All you ever talk about is going to some big stupid city."

"I know you're mad I'm helping people with grants. You judge every person who decides to leave."

Because maybe if we all refused to leave, the state would have to do something.

"Do you really think Louisiana is that bad?" There was plenty I would change about this state, but I couldn't imagine not loving its good parts. "Is that why you want to run away from it?"

"I don't want to run away from anything," Maddie said. "It's running toward something bigger. I want to live in a place with all four seasons. I want to sit in coffee shops and eat in nice restaurants and visit museums. I want to go to plays and concerts and do all the things that other people take for granted. And I want to live in a city full of beauty in a house that doesn't sway when the wind blows."

The beautiful parts of Boutin were the wild places, tucked down narrow canals and around bends in the bayou. Drive through Boutin by car, and you'd see faded buildings and rusted trailers and plain houses built high on stilts. You'd see yards with weeds and boats. Not fancy boats with gleaming hulls either. Work boats.

"So Boutin is small and trashy?" That meant she

thought I was small and trashy. "You sound just like those state people."

"That's not what I said." Maddie's face was flushed and her neck was splotchy, which meant she was very mad. That was fine with me—I was mad too.

"But if people would stay and fight instead of abandoning it—"

"What do you think Mina and I have been doing? Helping you fight!"

"But it shouldn't just be my fight—it's supposed to be ours! But you don't care that Boutin is disappearing because you think it's small and uncool. Maybe you're glad it's going underwater so you can leave faster." I whirled on Mina, who flinched a little at my face. "And you aren't even from Boutin. You don't know what it's like losing your home to the water."

I'd never seen Mina mad before, but I was pretty sure this was what it looked like.

Her easy smile was gone. "And you don't know what you're talking about," she said through gritted teeth. "You aren't the only person in the world who's lost something."

"We get that you're upset," Maddie said.

I was so sick of people using the word *upset*. I was so much more than that.

"But you're being kind of selfish."

The mad ate every single word I had in me. I grabbed my tray and stormed off. They didn't try to stop me.

Maybe I was more like my dad—he left when things got tough.

But even that thought didn't make me turn back.

I was curled up on my bed when Mama poked her head in the door. "Uncle Pete said the sacalait are biting."

"It's cold."

"Wear a coat."

I hadn't gotten any texts from Maddie or Mina in days. The silence in my room was almost overwhelming without Lucy's gentle snores or the *thwap* of her tail on my bed. I was still mad at Mama. But an hour later we were sitting in the boat, casting our lines out over the water.

"I think Uncle Pete is full of it," I muttered. I hadn't caught anything yet, though Mama had a couple of nice ones in the live well.

"He usually is. But sometimes you have the right bait, the right conditions, and they still don't bite. You work hard and still have nothing to show for it. Not everything in life is in our control."

"Are we still talking about fishing?" I didn't want to talk about anything difficult. I was tired of difficult. I just wanted to live in the tiny pockets of peace I managed to carve out of each day. I took a deep breath and jiggled my line. The water lapped against the boat. My tension relaxed its talons a bit. And Mama was fixing to shatter the stillness. "You're not supposed to talk while you're fishing."

"It's not like they're biting much anyway. I just wanted you to know that it's not your fault your dad left."

"I don't think it's my fault." Not completely.

"Well, just in case you do. Nothing he does is your fault." She jerked her line and stopped talking as she reeled, eventually pulling in a sacalait too small to keep. She frowned at it and tossed it back. "And I need to apologize to you."

I had not expected that. "You do?"

"I should have talked to you first. About moving. You matter more than anything else, and I shouldn't have just dropped that on you."

I sat with that for a minute as we drifted beneath the trees, a few draped with Spanish moss that floated in the breeze. It was hard staying angry out here.

"I had a fight with Maddie and Mina," I finally said.

"Do you want to talk about it?"

"They just don't understand." And I couldn't make them. It felt like I couldn't make anything happen, no matter how hard I tried. "Maddie wants to leave. And she's helping people with grants so they can leave too. And I failed at the school board office."

"You did everything you could at that meeting."

Had I? I felt like I'd screwed up my one chance. If I'd gotten the school board to agree, if I had a school in

Boutin to attend, then Mama probably wouldn't want to move. I failed and it all fell apart.

"You didn't fail."

"Of course I did! The school isn't reopening! And I just want things to be like they've always been and they aren't and I can't do anything about it."

"You put too much pressure on yourself. You can't expect to save the world."

"I wasn't trying to save the whole world—just my tiny corner of it."

We fished in silence for a while. I felt a tug on my line, and as badly as I wanted to pull, I waited a few more seconds before setting the hook. I reeled and pulled, fighting the fish as I hauled it closer to the boat.

"It's a keeper!" Mama said once I had it out of the water. I tossed it in the live well and rebaited my hook.

Would we still have these moments if we moved to Carolton?

"I don't want to leave Boutin," I finally said. How was I going to know if I was living up to the family name if I couldn't follow in their footsteps? I couldn't graduate from Boutin High or catch my limit on opening day of shrimp season or be buried with the rest of my family in Eternal Rest Cemetery. I would never peel shrimp at the Shrimp Shed or have the first crawfish boil of the season in my own backyard.

How could I be a real Robichaux if I didn't live in Boutin?

"I know. This was not an easy decision to make. But I can't stop what is happening, as much as I would like to, for your sake more than anything. Sometimes you rebuild, and sometimes you move on." She laid her pole in the bottom of the boat. "Caught enough?"

"I guess." I reeled in my line and tossed the bait into the water.

"Got your phone?"

"Yes."

"Good. Because even though you never asked, I have a story to tell on camera."

"I asked!" Hadn't I?

Mama just smiled. "It's a good one too. It's about the time me and some of my friends built a bonfire for Papa Noel and nearly burned half of Boutin."

The bonfires on the levee to show Santa the way here had been one of my favorite things as a kid. They'd stopped doing them this far south a few years ago.

"I can't believe Nonnie never told me this one!" I said.

Mama cranked the engine. "That's because Nonnie doesn't even know this one. My friends and I swore we'd take it to our graves. But it's a heck of a good story, and I think it deserves to be saved."

Chapter Seventeen

March arrived with warmer temps and azalea blooms. Boutin schools were still closed and would probably always be that way. Mama was looking at houses in Carolton, and Nonnie was promising she would live in her boat if she had to but she wasn't moving. I hadn't talked to Dad since he left, and there was a very noticeable Lucy-shaped hole in my life.

Maddie and Mina and I were speaking, but we weren't talking.

But I refused to be only hopeless and angry and anxious and frustrated. I wanted to enjoy my favorite parts of Boutin while they still existed. I had stories to collect and a project to finish. I focused on making the little bit of difference that I could because Mama said if we all made the world a little bit better one small act at a time, those acts would add up to more change than we ever dreamed possible.

We'd already volunteered to plant marsh grass before we had our fight. I'd kind of hoped that Maddie and

Mina would back out so that I wouldn't have to spend the majority of the day in forced politeness, but they hadn't, so one windy Saturday, Mama, Maddie, and I headed toward Carolton to pick up Mina.

Marshes were one of my favorite places. They were water and grass, fish and birds and wildlife, this whole colorful universe all their own. I loved sitting in a boat watching the wind ripple the grass as I waited for a bite on my line. Marshes were peaceful and promising and slowly disappearing. And I could help fight that. Despite everything else, I was pretty excited about the prospect.

Maddie sat quietly in the back seat. Mama tried to smooth things over but eventually quit after one-word answers from both of us. I'd been looking forward to this for a while, so I refused to let what happened with my friends ruin that. And yet. I wanted so bad to be laughing with Maddie. I wanted to hear all the trouble her little brother, Reed, had gotten into. I even missed her endless parade of facts. And I was dying to tell her about the birds that were building a nest right outside my bedroom window. I hoped I got to see their eggs hatch.

I missed my friends.

But I said none of that. Instead, I stared straight ahead and thought about marsh grass. Volunteering wasn't selfish, and I'd prove Maddie wrong.

Mina lived in an older neighborhood, and even though most of the Carolton I'd seen had cleaned up the flood debris, about half the houses here looked to be in the middle of remodeling. Mountains of debris sat on both sides of the road. Rolls of carpet and foam padding, jagged hunks of Sheetrock, broken cabinets, and shattered tiles and soggy cardboard boxes formed small peaks along the otherwise flat landscape. None of these houses were on stilts. This neighborhood wasn't ever supposed to flood.

White FEMA trailers squatted in several shaggy and neglected front yards. Mama checked the address, then eased over to the side of the road, where Mina waved to us from the top step of one of those trailers.

I went completely still as I stared at the pieces of Mina's house piled in the front yard. Not once had she talked about her house flooding. Not once had I asked. I'd just assumed she couldn't understand what I was going through and hurled her friendship back in her face.

"You ready?" I shouted as I hopped out of the car. I made my voice sound normal and carefree and not at all how I actually felt.

"Almost. My mom wants to say hi to your mom, and I need to get my camera from my room. Come on in."

Nonnie had promised to drive us around later so we could take more pictures. We were getting close to being done, and the Discovery Center seemed really excited.

We walked through a small living room and into the kitchen. Mina's mom was arguing with a little girl who had to be Mina's sister. She had the same infectious smile and bright eyes. "You are not building a ropes course in the empty house."

"But, Mom—"

"Nope. Go spend that energy elsewhere. Train the cat to dust or something."

The little girl wanted to be mad, but a giggle gave her away. She rolled her eyes and stomped outside.

"My seven-year-old is going on twenty-five," Mina's mom said.

Mama laughed. "I had one of those."

"And she's standing right here, so watch it," I said.

"You must be Jillian. Mina's told me all about you."

Oh, I really hoped not. Mina's mom said something to Maddie, but I couldn't hear her over the sound of shame ringing in my ears.

"Come on," Mina said, dragging me and Maddie away. "I'll get my camera."

We left the two moms talking—about us I was sure. The trailer was cramped, but I could tell Mina's mom had tried to make it look homey. There weren't any pictures on the walls, but she'd thrown bright pillows and blankets on the shabby furniture. Vases of flowers sat on scratched tables.

"I didn't know you flooded," Maddie said.

"It was kind of scary. Bayou Lafourche runs along the back of our house. The water came up pretty fast." Mina had her back to us as she led us down the short hallway, but her voice was a jangle of sorrow and anxiety.

“I’m so sorry,” I said. About so many things.

“Disasters happen.” Her voice was prickly and thorny. Mina stopped at the room on the left and flipped on the light. “I have to share a room with Kyra.”

The two twin beds could barely fit in the room. Mina’s side was combination photo album, science lab, and art project. A camera, printed photos, a microscope, colored pencils, and a book on painters cluttered the floor and end of the bed. The only organized part was the rows of different tennis shoes lined up against the wall. All of Kyra’s side was tidy. A stuffed elephant sat on her bed.

“That must be tough,” I said.

She turned to face us. “If I’m being honest, sometimes I hate it. I can’t wait to get my room back. But she needs me. She has bad dreams. We weren’t ever really in danger—the water came up and we got out—but it isn’t easy seeing the stuff that matters to you, that you care about, ruined. We lost all our books. Most of her toys. What we couldn’t get packed in twenty minutes got left behind.” She looked inside her camera bag before zipping it shut and slinging it over her shoulder. “Our cat slipped outside while we were running around and Kyra thought he’d drowned. We found him in a tree, but it was traumatic for a bit.”

“I’m a horrible friend,” I said.

“You asked why I wanted to help with the project. One of the main reasons was because we lost all of our pictures in the flood. So I think saving the ones we can is a really good idea."

"I am so sorry," I told her. "I shouldn't have said what I did."

Mina's face was serious for a bit, like she was weighing each individual word. Finally, she smiled. "Thanks for saying that."

"Have you even stopped to think about what people like my family will do?" Maddie asked. She was still mad, and I knew her enough to know that some of that was on Mina's behalf. Maddie liked to believe that she was practical and reasonable and guided by facts, but she was tenderhearted. Mina was hurting, and Maddie was mad because she couldn't do anything about it.

That was a kind of mad I understood.

"Aunt Nonnie owns her house. But my mom and dad don't, and nobody is going to buy a house in Boutin. But we still have a loan. My parents stay up late at night talking about it."

Which meant Maddie stayed up late worrying about it. And this whole time I'd only been thinking about me. Maybe Maddie was right. Maybe I was selfish.

"We can't afford to buy a new house somewhere else, so if we're going to leave, we're going to need a grant."

"Are y'all leaving?" I asked.

"Are we being given a choice? Stay and lose everything? Leave and lose everything? Just because I don't want to live here the rest of my life doesn't mean I hate it. It would be easier on me if I did. I feel guilty that I've always wanted to move and now the whole town has to. And you can be as upset as you want, but you can't take it out on us." And in her glare, I saw the resemblance between her and Nonnie.

She was right. "I'm sorry," I said again. I was saying it a lot, but I should have said it more, and sooner. I knew Boutin was more than the land. It was the people too, and Maddie saw that. There was more than one way to help.

"I'm sorry too," Maddie said. "You aren't selfish."

"I was being a little selfish." Sometimes the pain in your heart is so bad you can't see anyone else's. But these were my friends, and I should have looked harder. "And I shouldn't have gotten mad about the grant thing. It's pretty cool, what you're doing." Even if it wasn't what I wanted for Boutin.

"I got the idea from an article I read on Isle de Jean Charles and the Biloxi-Chitimacha-Choctaw people. Did you know they've lost, like, ninety-eight percent of their land?"

I shook my head. I'd only been worried about my land, my home. But of course other towns in Louisiana were sinking too.

"They're relocating their residents with grants. But some of them don't want to go either."

Of course they didn't. They'd built a community there, and then the oil companies dredged and the sea levels rose and now they were losing their home. It wasn't fair.

"Home doesn't just mean the place I stay. It's where I play and fish and dream. Where Papa's buried. I don't want it to disappear." I finally spoke my fear out loud. "Boutin is a part of me—what if that part disappears too?" What if I lost hold of my Robichaux if I moved to a town where they never lived?

"It can't," Mina said. "Look at everything you've done. You're creating an exhibit!"

"*We* are," I said.

"Right. But it was your idea."

"Yeah, so?"

"So you obviously believe that part of saving Boutin is saving its stories."

"So they don't disappear," Maddie said. "Which means that part of you won't either."

Home was a place. But what if home was also a story, a yarn, a whole world built of places and people and smells and memories all bundled together and tucked away in our souls?

"I hope you're right," I told them. I needed all my brave for what was coming. I sure hoped that wasn't a piece that disappeared. "But I know who I am in Boutin. I have no idea who I'll be in Carolton."

"Why in the world would you be any different?" Mina asked. "You go to school here now." She turned to Maddie. "Is she different?"

"Well . . ." Maddie tilted her head and examined me. "I think she's always had this temper."

"Places and people don't get to define you," said Mina. "You define you."

"I'm not ready to stop fighting."

"Good," Maddie said.

"Don't," Mina added.

"I want to make a difference." These were my friends, but still I flushed saying it out loud. Maybe my dad was right—that I needed to grow up and realize that I was thirteen years old and couldn't do much about anything. "I'm just . . ."

Just from south Louisiana, from a tiny, near nonexistent town, now too small even to qualify as that. I knew nothing about the world. There were so many people my age who had actually seen the world, done amazing things, been exposed to more in a month than I might be in a lifetime.

"Nope," Maddie said. "Don't you dare say you are *just* a kid or *just* a girl or *just* from Boutin. We are *just* as likely to do amazing things as anyone else."

"I'm certainly planning on it," said Mina.

Maddie leaned forward. "Have you ever thought that you're—we're—actually more able than most?"

"How?"

"Because this fight matters to you. To us. That's half the battle." Maddie grinned. "And because you might be the most stubborn Robichaux."

"Absolutely not. Have you met Nonnie?" Uncle Pete always said Nonnie was stubborn as a mule and twice as ornery. "Stubbornness isn't a talent."

"Sure it is," said Mina. "Most people quit trying before they find out what they can do."

"And I'm too stubborn to quit. Even if it's hopeless."

Maddie's eyes met mine. "You're stubborn enough to hold out hope."

I didn't deserve my friends, but I was so glad I had them.

Mina's little sister held up the departure by attaching herself to Mina and begging to come, but Mina's mom finally pried her loose with the promise of her own adventure.

My knees trembled and bounced pretty much the whole ride to Houma, but only because I was ready to get started. I'd wasted too much time not knowing.

The air was warm but hadn't yet taken on that muggy quality that was on its way. The azaleas added bright daubs of color everywhere.

"I don't know why I can't stay," Mama said.

"You sound like Mina's little sister," I told her.

She stuck her tongue out at me. "No one wants to be left behind." Her voice cracked. "Y'all are just growing up so fast."

"This is exactly why you can't go with us," I said.

I didn't want to feel like a kid playing pretend with the grown-ups. This was an important thing we were doing, with actual positive results. Mama wanted to move on; I wanted to stay and help.

She dropped us off half an hour later. A small group clustered in the parking lot. Maddie and Mina and I grabbed our water jugs and joined the knot of people willing to dedicate a Saturday volunteering.

"Bug spray and sunscreen, people," Dr. Nelson said. "Bug spray and sunscreen."

Mama had made sure we had both.

The group divided up into two boats and headed out into the marsh. After numerous twists and turns, I had no idea where we were and was thrilled I wasn't going to be in charge of getting us back.

The boat finally slowed down and eased into a canal. The banks on either side were mostly mud, though I could see some marsh grass sprouting up.

"Every clump of grass you plant keeps the canal from getting bigger," Dr. Nelson said as the boat came to a stop.

We climbed onto the bank.

"You just have to kneel down and shove the stalks into the mud," Dr. Nelson told us. "There's no clean way to do it."

Maddie and Mina and I might have been the youngest, but we sure were the first ones down in the mud. It immediately soaked through my jeans.

"Gross." Maddie wrinkled her nose. It smelled pretty nasty.

I giggled.

"Just like making mud pies," Mina said. She shoved her stalk of grass in the mud.

"Maddie never made mud pies," I said. "She doesn't like getting dirty."

"But I'm here." And she was already covered in the stuff. "I promise you I will have a job where I stay clean and indoors."

I didn't mind the mud. Even though we were a couple of hours from Boutin, this felt a little like home, surrounded by fresh air and sunshine and friends who were family. Maddie had mud on her nose. Mina's hat kept flopping in her face. Watching my friends plant the grass, I was so very happy I wasn't here doing this by myself. I was glad we were a team again.

It was slippery, so a few people were on their behinds before they knew what had happened. After ten minutes, I was completely covered in mud below the waist. I knew by the end of the day, I'd probably even have it in my ears.

"This acre of grass we're planting will grow to two acres by next year, then four the year after that. You are literally rebuilding Louisiana right now."

Dr. Nelson's words sent goose bumps down my arms. I was helping to save my state, but even better, I wasn't having to do it alone. Because this would take all of us.

We worked in small groups. Some of the people were

retired; others, scientists from the center. There were several college kids too, here as part of a course.

"So where are y'all from?" a woman asked. She was older than Mama but younger than Nonnie, her black hair streaked with gray and pulled into a ponytail.

"Boutin."

She shoved grass into the ground. Her arms were caked with mud up to the elbows. "Where's that?"

"All the way at the bottom. Where are you from?"

"Baton Rouge."

The capitol wasn't that far away, yet she didn't even know that my town existed. That meant no one was talking about our voluntary evacuation either.

"We're going underwater," I told her. Several other people were listening now. I talked about the flood, my school, the bridges.

"I had no idea," the woman said. "Well, I did or I wouldn't be here. But I thought that was a ways off still, definitely not something my generation would see."

It was just something my generation would live.

As dirty and hot and tired as I was, I was also filled with a fierce joy. This was what I wanted to do. Make a difference. Add to a place rather than take away.

Mama said the world should benefit from our existence, not suffer from it. I wanted to give back to this place, for everything it had given me. At the very least, this was how I started.

Maddie struck up a conversation about classes and

majors and advisers with one of the college girls. Mina had found someone else interested in photography and was using words I didn't understand. I wiped my hands on a dirty towel, mostly just smearing the grime, and took a water break.

"It's coming along," Dr. Nelson said. She had mud streaked across her forehead.

I nodded and took a drink of water, hoping it would unstick my tongue from the roof of my mouth. Dr. Nelson made me hopeful and nervous and shy.

"What does an ecologist do?" I blurted out.

"Lots of different ecosystems, lots of different ecologists. But my research is on the coast. We do work in the field, which means we go out to sites, like marshes and barrier islands. We do work in the lab, with microscopes and computers. We use a lot of science but also a lot of math."

It sounded hard. And wonderful—a bigger version of what I'd been trying to do since the flood.

"You try to protect and save the ecosystems." The word felt weird in my mouth, like trying on shoes I hadn't yet grown into. It was a big scientific word for home. Because that's what ecologists did too—they saved homes. Homes for animals and birds and fish and people.

It sounded like a way I could be there for a land that had always been there for me, a way I could help people from ever going through what I was.

"Your exhibit for the center—that's a really important thing you're doing."

It had always felt important, but hearing Dr. Nelson say it aloud made it feel like an even bigger responsibility. But . . . "I want to do more than save stories."

"You can. You know, we have a two-week summer camp for students your age. You can learn all about marshes, how they affect our environment, the effect we have on them, and what we can do to protect them. You should check it out. It's a residential camp, so you stay for the two weeks."

The mud cracked on my face when I smiled. "I would love that."

"Dr. Nelson!" One of the other scientists waved her over. I watched her check on groups, make notes, plant grass. She was doing. Helping. Saving.

She was exactly what I wanted to be in twenty years.

Chapter Eighteen

Nonnie was standing on the front porch when we pulled in. "Did y'all bring the entire bayou home with you?"

"Maybe." Mama had laid trash bags across the seats to keep them from being ruined, but mud had fallen off on the floorboard and I left a trail behind me as I walked to the porch.

"Run inside and wash up. We're running out of daylight, and if I'm going to talk on that stupid camera, we'll need to hurry."

I skidded to a stop. I hadn't mentioned it, not since the last time. I hadn't wanted to see so much anger and sorrow splashed across Nonnie's face again. I opened my mouth to ask why she'd decided to tell her story after all, but I chickened out and disappeared inside without saying a word.

We took turns in the bathroom. There was no time for a shower—I didn't want Nonnie changing her mind. I scrubbed my hands and face and put on clean clothes.

Maddie and Mina did the same, and in fifteen minutes, we were climbing into Nonnie's boat.

We pulled out of the backyard in the bateau and headed west. "I've seen the water come up over the years, but my grandfather wouldn't recognize this place," she said. "It really does look completely different from a hundred years ago."

We took pictures of the old dance hall. The wide-open water that used to be nothing but narrow canals and marsh grass. Fiddler's Point.

I wanted to capture all of Boutin before it was gone.

"Do you have that blasted video camera with you?" Nonnie asked.

Mina held up her phone. "Got it."

Nonnie looked out over the water, then nodded her head and started the boat.

"Where are we going?" I asked.

"You'll see."

She drove through bayous and canals. Nonnie had been adamant about not talking on camera, and I wondered what in the world had made her change her mind.

Mina pointed to neon flags sticking up out of the water. "What are those?"

"They mark pipelines," I told her. "Keeps people from running over them." Not that all of them were marked. Last year a couple of men ran over an unmarked pipeline and ripped a hole in their boat. They drowned.

They both could swim. But sometimes you don't get that chance. Sometimes the water just takes you.

Nonnie throttled back on the engine, slowing down as we reached an enormous live oak. Gnarled and black, its empty branches bent toward the water that had slowly covered its roots. Nonnie killed the engine and dropped the anchor to keep us stationary.

"Is this okay?" she asked me.

"It'll be fine."

Nonnie stood at the wheel, the tree dark and haunting behind her. Maddie, Mina, and I sat at the front of the boat.

"You ready?" Mina asked.

"As I'll ever be." She took a deep breath.

Mina hit record and pointed at Nonnie to let her know we were rolling.

"My oldest brother, George, was thirteen when I was born, out of school just as I was getting started. Growing up, I sat underneath this tree and watched him and a bunch of boys from town play baseball. Generations of Boutin's kids played here. Couples kissed behind the branches. If you could get close enough, you'd see my brother's initials, along with his sweetheart's, carved into the trunk near the roots.

"One summer evening after my brother and his friends had graduated high school, they gathered in this field to play ball, like they had a hundred times before, from the time they were old enough to swing a bat." Nonnie stopped looking at the camera and found me. "Sometime you'll have to get Uncle Pete to tell you the story about when Emile Gillespie broke his leg and they carried him the two miles into town. He tells that one better than anyone else who was there." She looked back at the camera. "My brother let me tag along. I was five and idolized him.

"He and several of the other boys had just joined the army. They were all going to basic in a few weeks, and though they didn't know it, that was the last night they were all together. The last time they played baseball. Several of their girlfriends had turned out to watch, some other siblings like myself, and I remember watching the game and chasing fireflies and playing tag with a couple of the younger kids. This whole area looked so different back then, the way the sun shone golden on the grass. Halcyon days, they call them."

Nonnie's voice had lost that rough rasp it usually had and taken on a softer quality. I could almost see Nonnie as a little girl, scraped knees and flyaway hair, as she chased after her older brothers. I could almost see her playing on ground that no longer existed.

"My brother was up to bat. I'd gotten tired of running around and had sat down to watch the end of the game. My brother had looked over at me and winked. 'For you, kiddo,' he'd said, and then he'd knocked the skin off that ball.

"At first I didn't know what it was. The ball shot over

the trees, gone, and my brother let out a loud whoop. Something white floated down from the sky, and for a moment I'd thought he'd knocked that ball so high he'd chipped off a piece of cloud. Then Danny Eckles shouted about his ball being ruined, and he held up the flapping white skin. My brother was laughing as he ran around the bases, which were two large flat rocks, one discarded coil of fishing line, and William Browning's hat.

"Of the fourteen boys who played ball that night, who watched my brother hit that ball into the marsh, only three of them made it past their twenty-fifth birthday. Most died in Vietnam, trekking through marshes not unlike where they'd grown up, not knowing they would never again see their homes. Not knowing that fifty years later, that home would be gone too, as much a memory as they are now."

Nonnie's story left a silence over us. Mina shut off the video and took a few pictures of the tree.

We sat in perfect stillness. An egret floated past. Most people would say there was nothing here. But this was my everything—everything I'd ever known and loved. Louisiana and its people had made and were still making plenty of mistakes. But I couldn't imagine sitting right here and believing this—we—weren't worth saving.

"Do you know anyone who has a picture of the tree when this was still land?" I finally asked.

"I might. We can go through the pictures later. If not,

there are a few people we could ask." Nonnie looked out over the water and watched the sun sink toward the horizon.

Once home, Nonnie went to the back porch, and Maddie and Mina and I went into my room. They were staying the night.

"I got dibs on the shower," Maddie said.

"Me next." Mina folded to the floor.

I was glad for my friends. The only thing missing was Lucy. Her absence made me heartsick. "I'll be right back."

"Everything okay?" Mama asked.

"She told us the story about George."

Mama's face shifted. "Ah. She's never even told me that one."

Nonnie was sitting on the top step of the back porch, cigarette in her mouth.

"I thought you quit," I said.

"In case of emergencies only," she said.

I sat next to her and leaned my head on her shoulder. She stomped out her cigarette and rested her head on top of mine. "Thanks for telling me that story." I hoped she heard all the words I didn't say. "And for talking on camera."

She gave me a little squeeze. "You're welcome. I decided I couldn't be a coward anymore."

Nonnie was the toughest person I knew. There was absolutely nothing coward about her.

"If you can be brave enough to talk in front of that school board, to keep fighting like you are, then I can be brave too."

I had no idea what to say to that. I didn't feel brave. I mostly felt scared and wobbly. But maybe that's what brave was—standing up despite the trembles.

Maybe I had enough Robichaux in me after all.

"George was worth remembering," she said. "Now he always will be."

We sat in silence and watched the night creep over the yard. Nonnie finally stood up to go in. "Now do some of that fancy editing you kids do these days and make me look like a movie star."

Chapter Nineteen

Shhhh, if you wake Nonnie up, you're dealing with her," I told Maddie.

Her mouth snapped shut like a bullfrog on a fly.

It was after midnight. We each had a blanket in one hand and a snack in the other. I eased open the back door, holding my breath for the squeak, but it stayed silent, and we stepped onto the back porch and into the night.

Frogs and crickets sang us down into the yard. Nonnie's bateau was tied to an old stump, and we climbed in, spreading the blankets on the metal seats. We lay on our backs and gazed up at the stars.

"This was an excellent idea," Mina whispered.

"I have them from time to time," I answered.

Maddie munched on popcorn. "We're almost eighth graders."

Seventh grade had flown by, maybe because I'd been so busy trying to change it. Time moves forward even if we aren't quite ready for it to.

"And then we'll be in high school," Mina said.

I would be the first person in my family not to graduate from Boutin. I'd imagined my future one way, and now I was having to readjust, imagine it completely different.

"I want to be an ecologist." It was the first time I'd said it out loud. It sounded too big.

Neither Maddie nor Mina seemed to think it was too big. They seemed to think it was just big enough. "Cool," Mina said.

"I can totally see you hip-deep in mud, hollering at your assistants," added Maddie.

I tried to picture myself grown, in rubber boots and a floppy hat, or a lab coat in front of a microscope, but that was too far away, and all I could see was me as I was now, standing on a soggy bank as the water kept rolling in.

"I'm going to be a doctor," Maddie said. And the thing was, probably 50 percent of kids said they wanted to be doctors. But Maddie really would be.

"I have absolutely no idea what I want to be," Mina said. "Because I want to be everything."

We laughed, because again, Mina probably would be. I could see her bouncing around from project to project, sprinkling her unique bit of glittery optimism on everything.

Maybe all of us could be more than one story, if we wanted to be.

"We have to tell our stories," I said. Our project was

due at the end of the week. We'd edited videos and snapped pictures and recorded stories. We'd preserved as much of Boutin as we could. And in two weeks we'd present at the Wetlands Discovery Center. Just thinking about it made me all jittery, so I spent most of my time not thinking about it. "And I think we should do it at the school."

We'd spent months gathering other people's memories, but this was our home too, and just because we hadn't lived here as long as Millie Lemoine or Bud Talbot didn't mean we didn't have our own stories.

"Boutin?" Maddie asked.

"Yeah." Other people told their stories about the places they'd loved that had gone under water. Well, our school had flooded, and we were the last ones who'd ever attend class there.

"You think they'll let you in?" Mina asked.

I stared up at the stars. The sky was a very big place. The world was a very big place. And maybe Maddie was right—maybe we did have just as much of a chance as anyone else to do great things. After all, the stars stared down equally on us all.

"Yes. I think they'll let us in."

Mama called the principal, Mrs. Melancon. They'd gone to school together. Mrs. Melancon had heard about our project and was willing to let us in to film.

"But you have to be in and out in an hour," she told us as she unlocked the gym door. We'd parked in the back so that no one would see us. I wondered if Mrs. Melancon was breaking the rules letting us in.

Mama came inside with us. We carried flashlights since they'd never turned the power back on in the building. They never would now.

The gym floor was trashed. The skinny strips of varnished wood were buckled and twisted, and we had to be careful not to trip.

"We were supposed to have the seventh-grade dance in here," Maddie whispered.

"We were supposed to have a lot of things," I answered.

We stepped out of the gym and into the hallway. A fine layer of silt coated the tiled floor.

"They haven't even tried to clean it," I whispered.

"They found asbestos," Maddie reminded me.

I was pretty sure the school was full of the stuff, but how could they have found asbestos when it didn't appear that anyone had been back in here? "It doesn't look like anyone tried to save it."

The hallways were dark, and what light that did manage to make it through the dirty windows was murky. A line of mildew ran along the wall to show how high the water had risen. It was past my knees.

"I had English in here," I told Mina as we passed Mrs. Fontenot's classroom. The colorful book posters she'd hung around her door had fallen off. The empty wall now looked sad and lonely. I could almost hear the bells signaling the end of class, kids shouting and laughing, Mrs. Hebert fussing people for running.

"Your dad and I snuck a few kisses back here," Mama said, pointing to the alcove near the cafeteria.

"Gross," I said. "Maybe you should have studied instead."

Her laughter filled the school. It would be the last time someone's did.

"You're probably right," she said. "But then I would have missed out on you."

Part of myself was splashed across these walls, embedded in the dirty and cracked floors. How much of me was I leaving behind?

"This was my locker." Maddie had stopped in front of the row of blue metal lockers. Rust bloomed across the lower ones. She spun the dial a few times to test it, then put in her combination.

It opened with a screech, and we all froze, listening. I didn't believe in ghosts, but if they did exist, I imagined it would be in a place like this. So many lives had been lived inside these walls. I couldn't imagine that kind of living not leaving some sort of impression behind. The hair rose on the back of my neck, but the hall stayed still and silent.

Mina shined her light inside Maddie's locker. Three Polaroids were taped to the inside of the door; all were mildewed enough that it was hard to make out who was pictured. Her books were swollen with moisture.

Maddie reached out and touched one of the books. It wasn't just a new school that we would have needed. It was also all new equipment and books. The library, small as it had been, was probably a total loss. Anything that hadn't been damaged by water had now been damaged by mold and mildew and neglect. The air conditioner had been shut off for months, and the school smelled.

"Remember last year when Derek left those cinnamon rolls in his locker?" Maddie asked.

I groaned. A hoard of fruit flies had taken up residence in the halls, and when the janitor traced it back to the source, they'd opened Derek's locker to discover the month-old cinnamon rolls.

"Seriously?" Mina asked.

That memory felt weird, like it had happened to a whole other Jillian, one who didn't know about floods and ruined schools and hometowns that drowned in hungry water. "Yeah. Ms. Pam in the cafeteria made awesome cinnamon rolls and he'd bribed some kids for theirs and then stuck the ones he couldn't eat at lunch in this locker for later and forgot about them."

"That sounds like something his dad would have done too," Mama said.

"Or the time Jeremy tried to flush his math cheat sheet down the toilet and flooded the entire hall?" Maddie said. "And that dang cheat sheet came floating right back up too!"

"It's a wonder this school survived as long as it did," I said.

"I just can't believe Mrs. Gates isn't going to scream at kids running to the lunch line anymore," Maddie said.

"Or that Mr. Russo won't sing Christmas carols the entire week before break."

"He did that when I was in school, too," Mama said.

I ran my toe along the floor, drawing a line in the dirt. "This feels like a wake."

Standing here and looking at what happened to the school, knowing the same thing was coming for Boutin, felt like trying to hold back the tide with my bare hands. I could clearly see the houses of families I'd known my whole life emptied out, floors covered in silt and leaves, walls buckled with moisture. Boutin would be a ghost town, and anyone who stayed behind would become ghosts themselves, trapped by memories of what Boutin had been, rattling around like bones in an abandoned tomb.

It felt like someone had punched a hole in my chest, and I regretted very much coming here.

"Figure out what you want to say," I said. "Pick a place you want them to see and a story you want them to know."

"I'll leave you to it," Mama said. She headed back toward the gym and Mrs. Melancon.

Maddie hovered near me, suddenly looking nervous.

"You don't have to talk on camera if you don't want to," I said.

“I want to.” She picked at the hem of her shirt. “Well, maybe I don’t really want to, but I’m going to. It’s important.” She gave me a quick hug, and I squeezed her back. “What are you going to say?”

“Honestly? I haven’t even decided yet.”

Maddie picked a spot and Mina set up her camera. I stood against the wall and gave Maddie a thumbs-up. The camera’s red light went on.

“This is the library,” Maddie said. She was standing in front of the double doors that led inside. “It was the only library in Boutin, and we shared it with the high school.”

It was dark behind her, but Mina stepped forward so the light from the camera could illuminate the swollen books and debris-littered floor. Dead computers sat on Formica tables. The librarian’s sweater still hung on the back of her chair.

“I spent a lot of time in here, doing research for classes, attending Beta and student council meetings. I’ve been dreaming about leaving Boutin for college ever since my parents took me to an LSU game and I saw a real college campus. I imagined myself walking between tall brick buildings and studying in a library with more books than I’d ever seen in one place. What I never dreamed was that Boutin would be the one to leave me. I always thought it would stay right here, ready to welcome me home during the holidays.”

Maddie jutted her chin out and threw back her shoulders. She always did that right before she tried bossing me around.

"I was planning on being president of student council next year. There were a lot of improvements I wanted to make at Boutin Middle. I'm sad I won't get to try.

"I did a lot of dreaming in this library. Now it's gone. I just want people to remember that it existed."

She took a deep breath and stopped looking at the camera. Looked at me instead. "Was that okay?"

Maddie might have been a Richard, not a Robichaux, but she still had plenty of Nonnie's grit. "It was amazing. I can't believe you did it in one take."

"It wasn't easy," she said, and her smile was sad.

I put my arm around her waist. "Nothing about this is."

"That was harder than I thought it would be," I told Mama after Maddie's and Mina's parents had picked them up. I'd filmed my story in the hall in front of my old science classroom. It had taken several tries before I'd gotten it right. I'd searched for the right words, and stumbled over the ones I found. I'd tried to be Robichaux-brave, but I finally had to let myself cry a little. My story wasn't just a goodbye to my school; it was a goodbye to the future I'd taken for granted. Now I knew it wouldn't look anything like how I'd imagined.

"I'm sorry." I could tell by her face that there was something else she wanted to say. My stomach fell somewhere around my knees. I was pretty sure I knew what it was. "I found a house," she said.

"In Carolton."

"In Carolton."

"And you bought it?" We rattled over a pothole, but even once the car had smoothed out, my insides felt like they were still jostling around.

"No. I wanted you to see it before I made a decision."

But her voice said she already had. She'd made the decision to move months ago, and nothing I'd done or said had changed that. "I thought we'd go check it out tomorrow after school."

This was really happening. We were really leaving Boutin.

Mama seemed to read my mind. "Just because we're moving doesn't mean you can't come back. It's not that far. Boutin will not disappear without you ever setting eyes on it again."

Mama slowed down and eased around the crumbling edge of road. The orange barricades were still up. The city had thrown some gravel in the hole, but it hadn't done much good. I wondered how long Boutin would be here to come back to.

The only house I could remember calling home came into view. Dad's truck was sitting in the driveway.

"What's he doing here?" I grumbled as Mama pulled in behind him. But then Lucy jumped out of the truck cab, and I forgot to be mad.

"Hey, girl!" I shouted as I got out of the car. I squatted down and she barreled into me, knocking me on my behind, covering my face with kisses. She danced away from me, barking and howling, then was back for more kisses. Tears pricked the back of my eyes—joy overflowing.

"I think she missed you," Dad said.

I was glad someone had.

"I'll leave you two to talk," Mama said.

I wasn't so sure I wanted to talk to my dad alone. I focused instead on scratching Lucy's neck.

"I'm sorry I haven't called," Dad finally said. "I was giving you time to cool off."

"What about all the other times you didn't call and I wasn't mad?" The anger fell right out of my mouth. Anger was heavy like that sometimes.

"I'm not a perfect father. I'm sorry I wasn't there for you when you needed me. While I was busy working and regretting, you grew up. And I missed everything."

If anger was heavy, hope was light, a helium balloon that floated right up to the top. I didn't want hope to show up like that, but it did. Because this dad sounded different than usual—like a man who realized he'd messed up. I hated how anger made me feel, all snarled up and prickly, and I didn't really want to be mad at my dad anymore. I wanted to make room for other things.

"I wanted to thank you for letting me stay here. I got

my house mostly finished now, and I was hoping you'd want to come and stay the weekend soon."

That was a bigger promise than I was willing to make. We had a lot of smaller steps between there and here. "Maybe." I'd done a lot of giving. If he wanted me to stay weekends, he would have to show me he'd really changed—that he was actually willing to show up when it mattered.

"How's the project coming along?" he asked.

"We're almost finished. The grand opening is in a couple of weeks, and we're presenting."

"That's really great!"

It really was. Or it would be if I weren't so terrified of talking in front of a room of strangers. One more familiar face might not be a bad thing. I could give him a chance to cross that chasm between us. I was willing to try out that special combination of bravery and kindness my mama had. I was willing to give him another chance. "You could come, if you wanted to."

His smile filled his whole face. "I would love to," he said. "There is this great seafood place there. Maybe I could take you to dinner afterward?"

I thought about Mrs. Millie's story about my dad. If I could be more than one story, maybe he could too. Maybe we just hadn't had the time to get to know one another yet.

Tiny steps forward.

"Sure. I'd like that." I squatted down and loved on Lucy one more time. I needed all the snuggles I could get.

Chapter Twenty

The drive to Houma was already a long one, but it felt even longer than usual. I twisted my fingers into complicated knots and bounced my toes until my knees whacked the console and both pain and my mama made me stop.

"Nervous?" Mama asked.

"It feels like my nerves are eating me from the inside out."

"You have absolutely nothing to worry about. You've already done all the work."

Mama knew a lot of things, but she obviously did not know what she was talking about. Collecting pictures and recording oral histories absolutely was not the same thing as standing up in front of strangers and giving a speech. Our project would be on display for the whole world to see. And though that had been our goal from the beginning, now it felt too big, too personal, like I'd forgotten to put on pants and everyone was looking.

I understood now why Nonnie hadn't wanted to

share her story. And I appreciated just how big an act it was that she finally did.

"Do you want to hear about your mama's first day of school now?" Nonnie asked.

"No." I'd never turned down a Nonnie story before, but I didn't need real examples of what nerves could do when they decided to gang up together. I already felt like I might throw up.

"I want you to know how very proud of you I am," Mama said.

"I haven't done anything yet."

Mama took her eyes off the road for a second to glance at me in the rearview mirror. "You're wrong about that. You've done so very much."

A little smidge of pride stomped my nerves down a bit.

Of course, they came screaming back when we pulled into the Discovery Center parking lot.

It was still early, so the parking lot wasn't full. My insides warred between hope that not many people would show up and fear that, again, not many people would show up. Mina and her parents and Maddie and hers pulled in right behind us. Dad wasn't there yet of course, but it was early. He'd be there. He'd promised, and although I knew he didn't always keep his promises, I had to believe he would keep this one. He knew, after the last couple of months, just how important this was.

He'd been there for his neighbors. He'd been there for Lucy. It was time for him to be there for me.

The director of the Wetlands Discovery Center, Ashley Martinez, met us at the door, and she looked just as likely to shimmy right out of her own skin as I was. She buzzed around us and clapped her hands. "I can't wait for y'all to see how it turned out!"

We'd sent the videos and copies of the pictures in last week. The exhibit wouldn't be completely done for a while, but they'd mounted a TV on the wall for the videos and framed and hung all the pictures.

I didn't feel so small as I stood in front of what we'd done. This was my idea. Our work. Our pictures. "We did this," I whispered to Maddie and Mina. They both looked just as proud and disbelieving as I felt. "We really did this."

Maddie's dad walked up and put his hands on Maddie's shoulders. "I'm so proud of you, kiddo."

Maddie seemed to grow two inches. "Thanks, Dad."

Both of Mina's parents were there too, bragging on the incredible pictures Mina had taken.

"You're not going to cry, are you?" I asked Mama.

"I'm thinking about it." Her voice sounded thick with tears already.

"You are not allowed to cry. I need someone steadier than I am."

"That's what nonnies are for." Nonnie winked at me as she walked up, and I breathed easier. I could always count on Nonnie to hold things together.

People continued to trickle in. Mrs. Martinez brought Dr. Nelson over. "Dr. Nelson is going to introduce you three. Then you just talk a little bit about the project. Once you're done, we'll turn the videos on and let them play. People can watch them, mingle, and talk. It's going to be great!"

She bustled off. Dr. Nelson was the calmest person in the room. "You've already done the hardest part," she said, but I wasn't so sure about that. The room was full. I'd seen Mrs. Fontenot and Mrs. Melancon, Willie and Janelle Guidry and Father Pierre and even Ida Labatut, whose son had brought her from Houston. I hadn't yet caught sight of Dad, but I also kept losing sight of Mama and Nonnie. There were a lot of people here.

Maddie and Mina huddled around me as we practiced again what we were going to say.

"We think you should be the one to talk," Maddie blurted out.

"We're all going to talk," I argued. "We all did this project." There was no way I could have done this all by myself.

"We did. We all worked very hard. But we'd just be repeating each other. Look at the room."

I'd been watching the room fill up with both familiar faces and strangers for half an hour.

"This matters," Mina said.

Of course it mattered. That was why we had to get it right.

"This needs to be good," Maddie said. "You're good. This was your idea. You saved those pictures and started this whole thing. We'll all stand up there, but you should say the words."

I had a lot of words to say. I just hoped they didn't get all tangled together on their way out. I also hoped they didn't pick up a hitchhiker. "Okay."

My phone buzzed. Dad.

My neighbor cut his hand on a saw and I have to take him to the hospital. Sorry about missing tonight. We'll do dinner soon.

I fumbled with my phone before getting it back in my pocket. Pushed my way through the crowd, out the back door, and onto the grounds.

The Discovery Center had wooden walkways over ponds and marshes, a whole outside educational area built to mimic Louisiana's wild places. I leaned against the railing and stared at the water, listening to the frogs croak.

I didn't know if I was madder at my dad or myself for believing him.

I'd held tightly to every crumb my dad had thrown to me, to those moments when he'd actually paid attention to me. I'd felt important when I'd made him laugh. I'd hoped he meant it about being sorry, about making more time for me. But he only meant when it was convenient—when he didn't have something better to do.

"Why aren't I enough?" I whispered to the water.

It was too stubborn to answer.

Dad had time for so many other people, but he didn't have time for me. What did that say about me?

Nothing.

The large windows of the Discovery Center glowed with golden light. Half of Boutin was in that room. They had always shown up for me. I had a community. I had a family.

"You're the one missing out." I wished Dad were here to listen. "I have Mama and Nonnie." And we had stories and shrimping, inside jokes and love that never ever had to be earned. "I haven't missed out on one single thing. And if you're too busy to notice I'm here, then that's your loss. Because you don't get to make me feel like that anymore."

I swiped at my face when I heard footsteps on the boards.

"Hey, baby girl." Nonnie leaned against the railing right next to me.

"Dad's not coming."

"I know. He texted your mom." We watched an egret float in and land on the opposite bank. "As much as I want to speak ill of your dad, he's your dad so I won't. I promised your mama that I wouldn't. But you are not the way other people treat you. Don't ever think that him not showing up tonight has anything to do with you. It doesn't. It has to do with him and no one else."

"I know." At the very least, I was trying to believe that. "I just—" I took a deep breath. "I wish I'd been born a Robichaux." Maybe then I wouldn't have to work so hard to prove I was one.

"I wasn't born a Robichaux."

I stilled. Of course she wasn't. I'd never really thought about it.

"I've been one longer than not. It's who I am. But it's not the only thing I am. And, honey, you are the most Robichaux of all of us."

"Robichauxs don't leave Boutin."

"Being a Robichaux isn't about where your feet are in that moment. It's where your heart is."

"I just want to be like you and Mama." Tough and kind and full of grit.

"Funny, I've always wanted to be like you. You are so full of hope and joy. You have such an enormous heart and an ability to see—and fight for—all the good in this world. You are the very best parts of all of us." She hugged me. "It's time to go in."

I might have been born a Landry, but I really wasn't anything like my dad. I chose not to be, and I showed up when it mattered. "I'm ready."

"You okay?"

The egret took off again, circling the pond and disappearing into the darkening sky. "I think I will be."

I let Nonnie lead me inside. Mama met me at the door. "I'm sorry."

My mama shouldn't have had to apologize for my dad. "You know, everyone tells stories about Dad helping his neighbors and in general being an awesome guy. But that's not the dad I know. Why can he be there for other people but he can't be here for us?"

She put her arm around me. "You can love him for the things he did right and be angry at him for the things he did wrong. People are complicated things, Jillie Bean, and our feelings for them can be complicated too. Sometimes he is a selfish jerk, and sometimes he isn't. It's as simple—and as complicated—as that."

Maybe my dad was a good man. But that didn't automatically make him a good dad.

Mrs. Martinez's face brightened as she caught sight of me, and she hurried to the microphone. "If everyone could find a seat please, we're about to start."

Mama gave me a quick hug before sitting down. Nonnie sat next to her and threw me a wink. Maddie's parents and little brother watched us expectantly. Mina's mom had to drag Mina's little sister into her seat.

Dr. Nelson came to stand beside us.

My entire body shook.

"Are you cold?" she asked.

It was cold in the building, but it was more that my body was mutinying. My bones were trying to shake and rattle me right out the door. My jaw was tense and tight and I worried I wouldn't be able to say any of the speech I'd planned.

The Robichauxs were fierce and strong, and I was a Robichaux. I could be just as tough as Nonnie. Just as brave as Mama. Just as stubborn as the two of them put together. I was all of those things, if I chose to be.

Mrs. Martinez nodded at Dr. Nelson, who walked up to the mic. "Good evening. I'm Dr. Evelyn Nelson, and I have the privilege of introducing three incredible young women."

Maddie Richard, best friend, cousin, smartest person I knew, stepped up to the mic. "I'm Maddie Richard. I'm a seventh grader at Carolton Middle."

Mina Davis, newest friend, artist, most positive person I knew, took her turn. "I'm Mina Davis, and I'm also a seventh grader at Carolton Middle."

I looked out into the crowd. My English teacher, Mrs. Fontenot, was sitting next to Mrs. Melancon. Maddie's and Mina's parents practically glowed, like they'd swallowed a bit of the sun. Mama seemed on the verge of floating right up out of her chair, and Nonnie looked like I'd already succeeded. A whole lot of people believed in me. I cleared my throat.

"I'm Jillian Robichaux. I started seventh grade at Boutin Middle, but I will finish at Carolton. This year I learned that Louisiana was going underwater. I heard about warming oceans and sea rise and coastal erosion. I learned that my hometown, where my mama and nonnie grew up, was sinking. That the place I love, where I fish and shrimp, watch sunrises and seasons, will disappear in my lifetime."

I was aware of the pictures behind me, the ones that showed a Boutin before and a Boutin after. One day, those pictures and videos would be part of the only things left of my home.

"I was angry and sad and shocked. And I wanted to do something about it. Since we couldn't save the land, we decided we could save the stories.

"I also learned that my school would never reopen, that the state would not rebuild the roads and bridges, ones that had been damaged for years and ones damaged during this flood. Boutin is under a voluntary evacuation. I have to leave.

"I know that most people outside this corner of the world might find it strange that I want to stay. Boutin is a tiny little place struggling to stay afloat—literally. Most people want noise and convenience. I want sunsets over the bayou and the sounds of frogs and cicadas."

Mama had bought the house in Carolton. There was no going back now. I looked at her. She was crying.

"We would like to thank you for coming here today. Maddie and Mina asked me to speak because this matters so much to me, but this should matter so much to all of us. This is our home, and we should fight for it. Because if we aren't part of the solution, we're part of the problem. My mama taught me that it's important to leave a place better than we found it. My nonnie taught me that stories linger long after we're gone. I hope what

Maddie and Mina and I have done accomplishes both. Thank you."

I wasn't shaking anymore. My bones weren't trying to rattle me out the door because in this moment, I didn't want to be anywhere else. It felt like someone had lit a fire inside my rib cage.

And then people were on their feet, clapping, and Maddie and Mina and I were grinning at each other.

Mama was the first person from the crowd to reach me. She didn't say a word, just wrapped me in the biggest, most Robichaux hug ever. Nonnie was next. Her hug included squeezes and back slaps. I got a lot of hugs after that, from Maddie's and Mina's parents, from Ms. Wilson and Ida Labatut.

Southerners hug a lot. Louisiana is really far south. So I think that means we hug more than most.

A man pushed his way through the crowd to us. "Stephen Singer." He shook our hands. "I'm from the Baton Rouge *Advocate*. My sister told me about this incredible group of middle school activists doing important things for our state."

I didn't feel like an activist at the moment. I felt more like a wobbly bowl of Jell-O.

But this meant people were listening. Learning. Our story was going to reach the state capital. Maybe from there other newspapers and websites would pick up on the story. It was what I wanted—for people to know, to care, to fight.

I wanted to know we weren't doing this alone.

Maybe I'd inherited some of Nonnie's story magic after all.

I stood near the TV while my video played. I hadn't watched it since Mina had filmed it, and I probably wouldn't ever watch it again, but I did want to see it this one time.

The deserted school looked even darker behind me as Mina's light shone on my face.

"My nonnie says that Robichauxs find their way home. When my grandpa's great-uncle got lost in the swamps, he found his way out. When my parents split up and my mama needed help, she went home and found it. If I ever lose my way, I'll have no home to return to. Boutin will be underwater."

A small crowd gathered around me to watch: Mama and Nonnie, Maddie and her parents, Mina, Mrs. Fontenot, the man from the newspaper.

"The purpose of videoing these stories is to ensure pieces of Boutin survive."

The video showed the empty hallway behind me.

"Once upon a time, this was a school where Boutin children grew up. Our mascot was the Pelicans. Once upon a time, there was a cemetery named Eternal Rest, but it couldn't last forever. My grandpa Frank Robichaux is buried there, and even though water will eventually cover his headstone, remember he existed. He could build anything out of wood. He hummed while he shrimped and danced in the living room on rainy days. Remember that the bells at St. Joseph's always rang after Mass and that the Shrimp Shed was the best place for gossip.

"When the water wins, please remember that Boutin once existed, that it mattered, that those of us who loved it will always call it home."

Chapter Twenty-One

I tossed an old pair of tennis shoes in a box and taped it shut. They were too small, but I just couldn't stand to throw anything else out. My bedding had been packed. My clothes were folded into laundry baskets and already in the trunk of Mama's car. Tonight I would sleep in my new bedroom in Carolton for the first time.

Mama knocked on the doorframe and stuck her head inside. "Need help?"

"I think I got it."

She and Nonnie had been going through the kitchen for a week, dividing out what belonged to Nonnie and what belonged to Mama. It wasn't easy, since everything belonged to *us*. We were a unit, a family, and separating our belongings when everything belonged to all of us had ended in furious silences and, sometimes, tears.

I'd laid on my bed and sobbed after I'd packed my first box, but the tears had dried as the boxes stacked up. Now I felt a curious sort of empty, all scooped out, like I was taking my body to Carolton but not much else.

Mama picked up my box of books and I grabbed a box of photos and birthday cards. All of the *me* had been packed up, leaving the room lonely and dingy.

The house looked smaller even though there were more empty spaces. My rubber boots weren't sitting by the back door. Mama's rain jacket wasn't hanging on the coatrack.

I added my box to all the others stuffed into the car. I had no idea where I was going to sit. Mama put her box in the back of Papa's truck.

"Nonnie's coming with us?" My heart began a hopeful trip along my rib cage.

"I'm helping you move," she said.

I hadn't noticed her sitting on the front porch. She was smoking a cigarette.

"Emergency?" I asked.

"Most definitely."

I didn't go back inside. Instead, I walked around to the back of the house and stood at the water's edge. Mama said I'd taken my first steps in the grass right here. We'd watched so many sunsets from this yard, caught crickets here, two-stepped with Papa here.

I knew I would be back to visit Nonnie. But it wouldn't be the same, because I wouldn't be living here. I wondered how long it would be until the water was to the back porch. How long would it be before the road from Carolton to Boutin went underwater? Before the bridge collapsed?

"I'm sorry," Mama said as she joined me. I heard the tears in her voice. "This isn't easy for me either. My whole life is in this house. I don't want to leave. But I will not be so afraid of change that I refuse to do what is best. You carry Boutin with you. Even when it's gone, as unfair and awful as that is, you'll keep it alive by remembering and sharing its stories."

"We're a family. We should stay together," I said.

"We are still a family, even if we live in different houses. Your nonnie may be stubborn, but she's practical too. She just needs time to adjust to this reality. She'll come around."

I hoped so.

"I have something for you," Mama said. She handed me a small black box tied with blue ribbon.

I untied the ribbon and lifted the lid. Nestled in tissue paper was a silver necklace, the pendant shaped like a teardrop. "It's beautiful," I said.

"It opens." She took the necklace from me and twisted the top away from the bottom. The inside was hollow. "I thought you could put a little Boutin in it. So you'd always have it with you."

"Thanks, Mama."

"You're welcome." She gave me a hug. "I'll meet you inside."

The wind lifted my hair from the back of my neck. A roseate spoonbill floated past, its wings dipped toward the sun. This would always be my hometown. No matter what happened, I'd always be from Boutin.

I bent down and scooped a tiny bit of dirt into the necklace. Screwed the top back on and fastened the chain around my neck.

I stood perfectly still, and in that moment, I thought I could feel Boutin's heart beating softly against mine.

Mama pulled into the driveway of our new house. Nonnie parked behind us, the bed of Papa's truck full of boxes. Uncle Pete was bringing a trailer later with the little bit of furniture we were taking with us, like my bed and dresser. Mama had to buy a new sofa and a dining room table. The furniture store was delivering those tomorrow.

I climbed out of the car. A dog barked. It was a very familiar bark.

"You have another surprise in the backyard," she said.

I raced around the side of the house. Let myself into the backyard through the gate. Was nearly tackled by a floofy ball of golden fur.

"Lucy!" I immediately threw my arms around her. She danced and barked and whacked me in the face with her tail. "What are you doing here?"

"Your dad thought you'd want her," Mama said, stepping out of the house and onto the back porch.

"Is he here?" Lucy ran to the back porch to get a pat from Mama, then hurried back to my side. She sank into a sit and leaned into my shoulder.

"No. He went back to working offshore."

"Wait a minute." I stood up and faced Mama. "He's giving me Lucy forever?"

"I think this is his way of saying he's sorry."

I looked down at Lucy, at her tiny cowlick and trusting face. "You don't say sorry by abandoning someone who loves you. She'll miss him, and she won't understand why he left."

But Lucy didn't know what I was saying. She just kept wagging her tail.

I would make sure she got all the walks and snuggles and games of fetch. When Dad had walked out on us, Nonnie had been there. I'd be there for Lucy.

"You and I have a whole lot of people loving us," I told Lucy as Mama went back to hauling boxes out of the car. "That makes us very, very lucky."

We walked into the house together. Lucy proceeded to sniff every single corner. I found Nonnie in the guest room, laying her grandma's quilt along the bottom of the guest bed. "You better not let that dog sleep in my bed while I'm not here."

"Your bed?"

"I said I wasn't moving away from Boutin, not that I wasn't ever going to drive across the town line." She straightened up. Her lined face still held sorrow, but she managed to lift one corner of her mouth in a half smile. "I'm going to want a sleepover every once in a while."

Mama stuck her head in the door. "Jillian, you have a letter."

"I do?"

"Yep."

"From who?"

"I guess you'd better open it and find out."

I didn't know anyone who would send me a letter in the mail. My name and Nonnie's address were written on the front. The Lumcon logo and address were in the upper left corner.

I tore into the envelope.

Jillian,

I thoroughly enjoyed working with you both in the field and on the Discovery Center project. We need more caring people like you fighting for this state, this planet. I wanted to remind you about the Summer Ecology Academy residential camp. It will be held July 15-30 at the Louisiana Universities Marine Consortium in Chauvin, Louisiana. I've included both a camp and scholarship application. You need two letters of recommendation, and I would be thrilled to provide one of those.

I skimmed the rest of the letter quickly, my eyes resting on the signature at the bottom of the page: *Dr. Evelyn Nelson*.

Two weeks living and learning about ecology and science and coastal erosion. Two weeks getting a glimpse into what I hoped was my future.

No one in my family had ever gone to college. But I wanted to.

Did that make me less of a Robichaux? I didn't think so. Because we have always loved the land, and this was just loving it in a different way. I was thinking maybe it was okay to be my own version of Robichaux.

I showed Lucy the letter. Let Mama and Nonnie read it. Hung it on the bulletin board in my new room.

Endings are very, very hard. But sometimes, they can also be beginnings.

Author's Note

I began writing this book after the flood of 2016. As in this book, our flood began as simply rain. I came home from work not realizing it would be a week before we went back. Some schools were out for months. Some schools have only recently been rebuilt.

As I write this note to you, Hurricane Ida has just passed. Places that I mention in the book, like Grand Isle and Houma, sustained severe damage. People are displaced, and some may never return home; sometimes the rebuilding is just too much.

Boutin is a fictional town, but the circumstances surrounding this story are very much real. Over the last hundred years or so, Louisiana has lost more than two thousand square miles of land. That's about the size of states like Rhode Island or Delaware.

So many people are working hard to combat this land loss. Some say it's too late, that Louisiana has reached a tipping point. I am not a scientist, and I do not know about that. I do know that doing something is usually better than doing nothing.

I love this land. Nature is a healing place for me, and I crave being outdoors. I was raised to leave a place better than you found it. And like Jillian's mama, I believe small acts can lead to great change.

We just have to work together.

Acknowledgments

When I was a child and envisioning how books were written, I imagined an author working in solitude until a book was finished. As it turns out, that is not how books are written. We do not do it alone, and I am so grateful for everyone who has helped this book along.

This book would not exist as it is without my amazing agent, Alice Sutherland-Hawes of ASH Literary. She saw the potential in this story and helped guide me into making it what it is today. I am so lucky to have her as an advocate for my work.

Thank you to Chloe Seager of Madeleine Milburn for answering my numerous questions during the contract phase. You have the patience of a saint.

I am so grateful for Megan Abbate, who loved and acquired this book. Thank you to my editor, Kate Meltzer, and to Emilia Sowersby, for your insight and guidance. You pushed me to make this story even better, and I am so proud of the work we've done.

Thank you to Alisha Monnin for this stunning cover, and to the amazing team at MacKids and Roaring Brook Press—Connie Hsu, Kathy Wielgosz, Kat Kopit, Jennifer Healey, Trisha Previte, and John Nora.

My critique partners Abigail Johnson and Kate Goodwin have stuck with me for years now, and I could not have traveled this road without them. I am so grateful for their helpful (and always spot-on) notes, for their phone calls and texts, for their enthusiasm and support that fills me with the hope I need to keep at it. Y'all are the absolute best. I mean it.

Reynold "Ray" Adams, thank you for answering all of my questions about shrimping and for sharing your stories. Thanks to Kathleen and Bonnie Sonnier, who helped with the Cajun French. Any mistakes are my own.

My parents have always supported and encouraged me, and I am ever grateful. My grandmother taught me to read, so it is definitely her fault I spend more money on books than clothes. My sister is absolutely the most supportive sister a human could ask for. Thanks for believing in this story (and me).

As always, thank you to my amazing husband. You never once doubted.